Fearless Female

SOLDIERS, EXPLORERS, AND AVIATORS

Sacagawea

SHOSHONE GUIDE, INTERPRETER, AND LEADING MEMBER OF THE CORPS OF DISCOVERY

KATIE GRIFFITHS

Cavendish Square
New York

Published in 2018 by Cavendish Square Publishing, LLC
243 5th Avenue, Suite 136, New York, NY 10016

First Edition

CPSIA Compliance Information: Batch #CS17CSQ

All websites were available and accurate when this book was sent to press.

Library of Congress Cataloging-in-Publication Data

Names: Griffiths, Katie, author.
Title: Sacagawea : Shoshone guide, interpreter, and leading member of the Corps of Discovery / Katie Griffiths.
Description: New York : Cavendish Square Publishing, [2018] |
Series: Fearless female soldiers, explorers, and aviators |
Includes bibliographical references and index.
Identifiers: LCCN 2016054485 (print) | LCCN 2016054781 (ebook) |
ISBN 9781502627476 (library bound) | ISBN 9781502627483 (E-book)
Subjects: LCSH: Sacagawea–Juvenile literature. |
Lewis and Clark Expedition(1804-1806)–Juvenile literature. |
Shoshoni women–Biography–Juvenile literature. | Shoshoni Indians–Biography–Juvenile literature.
Classification: LCC F592.7.S123 G75 2017 (print) | LCC F592.7.S123 (ebook) |
DDC 978.004/9745740092 [B] –dc23
LC record available at https://lccn.loc.gov/2016054485

Editorial Director: David McNamara
Editor: Stacy Orlando
Copy Editor: Nathan Heidelberger
Associate Art Director: Amy Greenan
Designer: Stephanie Flecha
Production Coordinator: Karol Szymczuk
Photo Research: J8 Media

The photographs in this book are used by permission and through the courtesy of:

Cover Edgar Paxson/Peter Newark American Pictures/Bridgeman Images; p. 4 Witold Skrypczak/Alamy Stock Photo; p. 7 Newell Covers Wyeth/Peter Newark American Pictures/Bridgeman Images; p. 8 Benedicte Wrensted/NARA; p. 13 AF Fotografie/Alamy Stock Photo; p. 15 Universal History Archive/Getty Images; p. 19 Ted Streshinsky/Corbis/Getty Images; p. 30 M L Pearson/Alamy Stock Photo; p. 33, 37 Buyenlarge/Getty Images; p. 41 American Stock/Archive Photos/Getty Images; p. 42 Library of Congress/Wikimedia Commons/File:Moenitarri warrior in the costume of the dog danse 0056v.jpg/Public Domain; p. 44 Stanley Meltzoff/National Geographic Creative/Bridgeman Images; p. 49 Charles Marion Russell/Texas Humanities/Wikimedia Commons/File:Lewis and clark-expedition.jpg/Public Domain; p. 52 Nancy Carter/North Wind Picture Archives/Alamy Stock Photo; p. 56 Interim Archives/Getty Images; p. 59 Robert Cicchetti/Shutterstock.com; p. 65 Macduff Everton/Corbis/Getty Images; p. 68 Kushch Dmitry/Shutterstock.com; p. 72 Graham Corbett/Getty Images; p. 75 Loomis Dean/The LIFE Picture Collection/Getty Images; p. 77 Edward S. Curtis/Underwood Archives/Getty Images; p. 82 Stan Honda/AFP/Getty Images; p. 90 Vladimir Wrangel/Shutterstock.com; p. 95 Julie Alissi/J8 Media; p. 97 United Archives GmbH/Alamy Stock Photo; p. 99 Lee Foster/Alamy Stock Photo; p. 109 Jamie McCarthy/Getty Images.

Printed in the United States of America

Contents

one

Early Settlers and the Dream of the West

"[Many] portrayals [of women like Sacagawea] emanate from non-Indian perspectives; they neglect Native context and deny the considerable influence these women wielded on both sides of the cultural divide."
—Rebecca Kay Jaeger

Histories involving **Native American** figures are often hugely complex. They are open to stereotyping, misinformation, and biased retellings from non-Native perspectives. If the history of fearless women can be said to have been in the past overwritten by men, the same is

Opposite: This statue of Sacagawea and her son appears at the Sacajawea Interpretive, Cultural, and Education Center in Salmon, Idaho.

doubly true for Native American or First Nations women. Their stories have been subject not only to male perspectives and prejudices, but to European and **indigenous** ones. One such woman is the famous Native American interpreter and keystone of American mythology: Sacagawea.

Sacagawea was a **bilingual** Shoshone Native American woman who spoke Shoshone and Hidatsa, two very different Native languages. She lived during the eighteenth and nineteenth centuries. From 1805 to 1806, she accompanied the Corps of Discovery expedition, led by Captain Meriwether Lewis and Second Lieutenant William Clark, from the northern plains through the Rocky Mountains to the Pacific Ocean and back. Her primary mission during the journey was to act as translator and informal peace ambassador, and her knowledge of parts of the more difficult terrain was invaluable. Her presence was used to reassure the Native American tribes they encountered that the band was not a war party. Throughout this arduous journey, she was also caring for her son, who had been born just two months prior to the expedition departing.

She is a woman who has been **mythologized** by American history to such an extent that it can be hard to find the real person underneath her story. Most accounts of her life were written by white **colonizers**, each with their own agenda and interpretation of her personality and actions. Debates continue to rage within academic circles over how big a role she played in the expedition and to what extent contemporary writers have hijacked her memory. Either way, it is clear that Sacagawea was a strong and capable figure who made significant contributions to the Corps of Discovery's work. However, to understand her importance and her character,

In paintings of Sacagawea with explorers Lewis and Clark, she is frequently portrayed actively directing the expedition's movements.

it is vital to first understand the context in which she grew up and became involved in the expedition.

The Lemhi Shoshone

The term "Indian" has often been used to describe Native Americans and is as common as it is misleading. The debate around terminology for American indigenous peoples, sometimes referred to as the "The Native American Name Controversy," is a complex issue and an ongoing discussion. Names differ according to region, age, tribe, and history, and

Lemhi Shoshone tribe members from southeastern Idaho in traditional and western dress

a majority of tribes prefer to be known by their specific nation or tribal names, which are occasionally open to debate.

In the 1960s, both Native American and non-Native people began to challenge the use of the term "Indian." It was argued that it was an oppressive title and also completely wrong. After all, the name was coined by Christopher Columbus, who, when he reached America, mistakenly believed he had landed in the East Indies. Critics also argued that the connotation of "Indian" had become so saturated in the racist imagery of Western films, books, and television shows that it had become an offensive reference that simplified and degraded a complex and diverse people. It was during this time that the term "Native American" was suggested as a replacement in order to reflect the fact that the people it referred to were the original inhabitants of America.

However, a large number of indigenous people have also rejected the "Native American" designation. In 1998, Lakota activist and founder of the American Indian Movement (AIM) Russell Means stated in his essay "I Am an American Indian, Not a Native American!":

> I abhor the term Native American. It is a generic government term used to describe all the indigenous prisoners of the United States ... I prefer the term American Indian because I known its origins ... As an added distinction the American Indian is the only ethnic group in the United States with the American before our ethnicity. At an international conference of Indians from the Americas held in Geneva, Switzerland, at the United Nations in 1977 we unanimously decided we would go under the term American Indian. We were

> enslaved as American Indians, we were colonized as American Indians, and we will gain our freedom as American Indians and then we can call ourselves any damn thing we choose.

Other Native writers and critics have argued that neither term is useful or correct. In *What's in a Name?: Indians and Political Correctness*, Cherokee writer Christina Berry maintains that people should avoid using both the terms "Indian" and "Native American":

> In the end, the term you choose to use (as an Indian or non-Indian) is your own personal choice … Very few Indians that I know care either way. The recommended method is to refer to a person by their tribe, if that information is known. The reason is that the Native peoples of North America are incredibly diverse. It would be like referring to both a Romanian and an Irishman as European. It's true that they are both from Europe, but their people have very different histories, cultures, and languages. The same is true of Indians … So whenever possible an Indian would prefer to be called a Cherokee or a Lakota or whichever tribe they belong to. This shows respect because not only are the terms Indian, American Indian, and Native American an over simplification of a diverse ethnicity, but you also show that you listened when they told what tribe they belonged to … What matters in the long run is not which term is used but the intention with which it is used.

The term "First Nations," which first came into use specifically in Canada, has also been more widely applied to all North

American indigenous people. With this in mind, this book will refer to specific tribes where possible, and will use the terms "Native Americans," "First Nations," and "American Indians" when describing the populations as a collective.

Coyote and the Creation of the Shoshone

Before Sacagawea's lifetime, her Lemhi Shoshone tribe lived in the Great Basin between the Sierra Nevada and the Rocky Mountains in western North America. The tribe was sometimes referred to as the "Snake People" by other Plains tribes because in Native sign language the gesture the Shoshone people used to refer to themselves meant "snake" to other indigenous peoples. However, among the Shoshone people, the sign actually meant "salmon," a fish largely unknown to the Great Plains. The vast tribe was widespread across the West, and while the different bands shared many cultural similarities, only the eastern branch of the Shoshones adopted a Great Plains way of life. The Eastern Shoshones divided into two groups, based on their location and resources. Shoshone bands living in the Green River and Wind River valleys of modern-day Wyoming were known as the Buffalo Eaters, or Sage Grass People. Bands living in the Rocky Mountains and Lake Yellowstone areas were called the Sheep Eaters, or Mountain People.

The Shoshone calendar followed circles of activity, trade, and travel. In the winter, the tribe would separate into bands depending the location they wished to travel to. In spring, the bands would reunite and move to the bison grounds to hunt. In summer, the tribe would relocate to the Wind River valley, and an intertribal gathering was held for the purpose of trade. After the gathering, the tribe would once more break into bands before rejoining for the fall hunt, after which the Shoshones would begin the cycle again.

The tribe was organized under the guidance of a chief, usually an older man who had gained a reputation for himself through warfare and was believed to have supernatural powers. He controlled tribal hunts and movement. During times of war, a special war chief would be chosen. Within Shoshone society, there were two military groups: the Yellow Brows and the Logs. The Yellow Brows were young men who were the first ranks into any battle. The Logs tended to be older warriors who would act as a rear guard during conflict. Both groups also acted as the tribe's police force during tribal gatherings.

Some historians believe that the Shoshone tribe originated in Mexico, hundreds of years before Sacagawea was born, but the creation stories of the tribe maintain that the Shoshone people's ancestors first began life in the Great Basin, near the Salmon River valley. The tribe believed they were descended from the mythological figure Coyote. He was both a trickster and a cultural hero who appears in many traditional Native American tales. One popular story of how the Shoshone descended from Coyote, retold by scholar Rebecca Kay Jager in her book *Malinche, Pocahontas, and Sacagawea: Indian Women as Cultural Intermediaries and National Symbols*, goes as follows:

> Coyote was led to an island by a young girl. Coyote feared her because she and her mother had teeth in their vaginas, and he thought they planned to devour him. He snuck off to retrieve his tools and returned to knock out their teeth so he could have sex with them. After intercourse he was told to go out and retrieve

The mythological trickster Coyote can be found in many Native American tales.

water. In his absence many babies (Indian peoples) were born. When Coyote returned he was told to wash the last two babies with the water he brought, but he did not. Had Coyote washed them, all of the children would have been the same. The two who had been separated from the rest, became Shoshones. Coyote told his Shoshone children to be brave and not to fear other Indians, who would always be against them.

The story of Coyote is quite revealing. Not only does it show the Shoshone connection and inheritance to the land, but it also attempts to explain diversity and even animosity among Plains Indians. In fact, the Shoshone tribe, and in particular Sacagawea's band, was an isolated nomadic group. While Sacagawea was still a child, in the late 1780s, her group was forced to retreat farther and farther into the mountains. This was for two reasons: firstly, for protection from European diseases that were beginning to decimate the First Nations population; and secondly, to avoid encroaching on the hunting lands of their more powerful and better-armed neighbors.

Neighbors and the Wider Community

The Great Plains region was not only home to the Shoshone tribe. Many other groups lived in the area. Their existence was largely independent of each other, but membership was fluid and members of one band were free to join another. This intermingling created a multiethnic community that occasionally fought each other but more often came together for trade, hunting, and war excursions.

Shoshone culture had great influence within the region and helped to increase diversity. They were among the first to

Plains Indians traveled annually to large gatherings for trade and to discuss political issues.

adopt different survival strategies to improve their standard of life. The tribe combined food-gathering methods of the Great Basin with hunting methods of the plateau tribes to the east. They acquired horses from the Comanche people, who lived on the southern plains, and American explorers Lewis and

Shoshones lived off fish caught from mountain streams, native roots and seeds, wild vegetables and fruit, and the occasional buffalo.

Gender and Economy

Children growing up in Shoshone culture followed fairly traditional paths. Boys were trained to be hunters and warriors. Girls were taught to gather food, sew, and care for babies. As a child, Sacagawea would have learned how to find and prepare over one hundred edible plants, such as the camas lily, which the Shoshones would prepare by drying out its potato-like bulbs. However, women were still involved in both hunting and trading.

The introduction of the new economy caused major shifts both in daily Native life and in the gender balance of work. Access to European trade made the horse-and-hide industry increasingly competitive. Hunting went from an act of subsistence and low-level trade to a high-profit machine. The introduction of horses to the plains had created more social mobility within tribes. A Shoshone man's status had been traditionally measured by his ability to hunt, his success in war, and his generosity. Now, being a skilled horseman could also increase his social standing and bring in greater wealth based on his ability to hunt large numbers of game. Hunting thus became an even more masculine activity.

The increase in hunting led to an almost instant need for greater numbers of people to help process the kills. Female participation quickly shifted to cleaning and preparing, rather than active involvement in the hunt. However, a mounted hunter

Shoshone women were responsible for the home and its upkeep, as well as being a vital part of the horse-and-hide economy.

brought in more animals than one wife could easily prepare. More females were needed, and soon polygamy, the practice of taking multiple wives, became common within the tribe. As scholar Rebecca Kay Jager argues:

> In an environment racked with increasing competition, disease, and warfare, men were declining in numbers and polygamy was a strategy for the preservation of the group. Some scholars have argued that nomadic Plains women lost prestige during this transition because they were no longer involved in the hunt, nor were they decision makers in trade because white traders preferred to barter with Indians men. However it is important to recognize that Plains women remained critical producers who were **indispensable** to the horse-and-hide economy.

Though women's status within Native American tribes was lower during this period, a fact not helped by the male European traders' obvious disregard for negotiating with women, they were indeed indispensable to daily life in the horse-and-hide economy. During Sacagawea's lifetime, demand for domestic labor was high. Women were trained in many different tasks, such as processing hunt kills, dressing the skins, drying meat, hauling wood and water, gathering and preparing food, rearing children, and crafting moccasins and other apparel. Women were also responsible for preparing the mobile village for its next move. This involved packing, carrying, and unpacking all the essentials of village life, such as tepees and cooking equipment. All of this was considered women's work despite its highly physically demanding nature. In Plains American Indian society, women owned and controlled the home and its contents. They were responsible for caring for and carrying all associated items in order to leave the men free to pursue enemies or game. Europeans who came across the tribe often recorded their amazement and dismay at the heavy work done by Plains Native American women. During Sacagawea's time with the Shoshone tribe, both Sacagawea and her female relatives experienced a life of constant movement, hard work, hunger, death, and uncertainty.

President Jefferson and Native Americans

At about the time Sacagawea reached her teenage years, the United States had reached its third president, Thomas Jefferson. He was one of the Founding Fathers of America and a keen advocate of democracy and republicanism. As president, he had a major impact on the country's First Nations peoples. During his presidency, he pursued a twofold "Indian policy" in regards to the indigenous population. He wanted to guarantee the security of the country by binding the Native American tribes to the United States through treaties. This would prevent them from siding with European powers such as England in Canada, or Spain in Florida, the Gulf Coast, and areas west of the Mississippi.

"Civilizing" the Natives

President Jefferson also wanted to use these treaties in order to gradually "civilize" Native Americans. By "civilize," he meant that he wanted Native Americans to take up European farming practices, give up the nomadic lifestyle, and allow the US

Geography of the Great Plains

The Great Plains region was the traditional homeland of the Shoshone tribe. This area is a huge expanse of flat land, covered in prairie, steppe, and grassland. It lies west of the Mississippi River and east of the Rocky Mountains, covering parts of Colorado, Kansas, Montana, Nebraska, New Mexico, North Dakota, Oklahoma, South Dakota, Texas, Wyoming, Minnesota, and Iowa, as well as the Canadian provinces of Alberta, Manitoba, and Saskatchewan. The Canadian portion of this territory is known as the Prairies. Some geographers have historically included some of northern Mexico in the Great Plains' borders, but most stop at the Rio Grande. Despite its large area, it is in fact only a subsection of the even vaster Northern American Interior Plains. These extend east toward the Appalachian Plateau. The region is most commonly known for supporting extensive cattle ranching and dry farming.

The Great Plains region has a particularly dramatic climate and a wide variety of weather throughout the year. Its winters are very cold and harsh, while its summers are humid and extremely hot. Wind speeds are high, especially during the winter. The region, especially in the High Plains, periodically experiences droughts, resulting in devastating dust storms. Throughout the spring and summer seasons, the plains are also vulnerable to thunderstorms. The southeastern section of the Great Plains is the most active tornado area in the world and is sometimes referred to as Tornado Alley.

Today, the Great Plains are most commonly broken down into ten different subdivisions: the Missouri Plateau, **glaciated**; the Missouri Plateau, unglaciated; the Black Hills; the High Plains; the Plains Border; the Colorado Piedmont; the Raton; the Pecos Valley; the Edwards Plateau; and Central Texas. As western expansion developed after the Louisiana Purchase, much of the area's prairies were eventually turned into agricultural areas or pastures.

government to take control of hunting grounds to facilitate further white settlement. While narrow-minded notions of what was civilized played a significant part in the creation of this policy, it was white settlers' desire for land that was the driving force behind it. Jefferson's methods for acquiring land were also extremely troubling. While he instructed his agents never to force Native Americans to sell their land, he did however suggest the use of financial manipulation. In one letter to William Henry Harrison, a military officer and the future ninth president, Jefferson suggested encouraging Native American people to purchase goods on credit so that they would eventually fall into debt and have to sell their lands to the government to recoup the losses.

Today, Jefferson remains a complicated figure in history. He consistently argued that he believed the Native American peoples to be "in body and mind equal to the white man," and in his book *Notes of the State of Virginia* he defended Native American customs and culture. Yet, he developed plans that would eventually lead to the forced removal of Native

The Emergence of Political Parties

Between 1792 and 1824, the United States saw the birth of arguably the world's first modern political party system. What made it so unique was the fact that the system was based on voters, rather than factions of aristocrats at court or parliament. This system saw two national parties, the **Federalist** Party and the Democratic-Republican Party, competing for control of the presidency, Congress, and individual states. The Federalist Party was established by Alexander Hamilton in 1789. Its supporters included John Jay, John Adams, Charles Cotesworth Pinckney, and Rufus King. They believed that an American national government should be strong, protective of economic growth, and keen to maintain diplomatic ties with Great Britain rather than revolutionary France. Its original members were bankers and businessmen who supported Hamilton's economic policies. These included a national bank, a federal assumption of state debts contracted during the Revolutionary War, tariffs to pay off those debts, and the national encouragement of banking and manufacturing industries. It appealed strongly to the business community.

Republicans, on the other hand, targeted planters and farmers. The party was created in 1779 by Thomas Jefferson and James Madison in an attempt to counter the centralizing policies of the Federalist Party. Among its more famous supporters were James Monroe and Andrew Jackson. Modern historians refer to Democratic-Republicans, or Jeffersonian Republicans, as the first Republican Party. In contrast to the

Federalists, the party opposed strong executive power, was hostile to a standing army and navy, demanded a more limited reading of the constitutional powers of the federal government, and strongly opposed Hamilton's financial policies. They were also deeply suspicious of British aristocratic influence and favored stronger political ties to revolutionary France.

Americans from their own lands. He firmly believed that such methods were all for the common good, perceiving these actions as a way to educate Natives in **Enlightenment** values while benefiting white interests. To his mind, forcing First Nations people to adopt European lifestyles would ensure quick evolution from "savagery" to "civilization," revealing his own Eurocentric notions of the correct way to live. By the beginning of 1803, his private letters revealed stronger and stronger support for a policy of First Nations removal.

Native Reactions

During this period, Native Americans were divided on how to respond to Jefferson's policies. Some embraced the program, such as the Shawnee chief Black Hoof who settled many of his people within the state of Ohio, where they became farmers. In the South, five Native American nations accepted the program and became known as the Five Civilized Tribes. Many members of the Creek and Cherokee Nations built towns and plantations, some even owning African American slaves like their white neighbors.

Others fought back. The Shawnee war leader Tecumseh headed the formation of a **pan-American Indian** resistance movement against the United States government in the years leading to the War of 1812. Many other southern Native American nations were also suspicious of Jefferson's plans and joined the pan-American Indian movement. Among the Creek Nation, an antiwhite resistance movement known as the Red Sticks rose against the United States and the Creek Nation itself during the War of 1812.

The Louisiana Purchase

A seismic event that would alter the course of Sacagawea's life happened in 1803. At the beginning of the nineteenth century, Jefferson wanted to secure access to the French-controlled port of New Orleans. He knew this crucial place would help to grow American industry by making goods easier to move. At the time, France was fighting on several fronts: a national financial crisis, a slave revolt in Haiti, and a looming war with Great Britain. The naval blockades that Britain had placed against France were slowly depleting the country. If Napoleon Bonaparte, soon to be the emperor of France, wished to fight against the British, he needed funds quickly. In April 1803, Robert Livingston, United States minister to France, was attempting to negotiate with French authorities in Paris to purchase New Orleans. Jefferson was already unhappy with the idea of the French increasing their power and control within the region, and he had previously warned Livingston that "[t]he **impetuosity** of [France's] temper, the energy and restlessness of her character, placed in a point of eternal friction between us, ... render it impossible that France and the US can continue long friends when they meet in so irritable a position." He also stated that the day France took full possession of New Orleans would seal the United States' political alliance with Great Britain—a stance that many in the Federalist Party, which was in opposition to Jefferson, were already arguing for back home. Therefore, Livingston was surprised but interested when questioned by the French as to whether the United States would want to purchase the entire Louisiana Territory. This area contained land that would later form Arkansas, Missouri, Iowa, Oklahoma, Kansas, and Nebraska, as well as large portions of Minnesota, North and South Dakota, New Mexico, Texas, Montana, Wyoming, Colorado, and of course the future state of Louisiana.

France had controlled the region since 1699. At the start of the seventeenth century, France had explored the Mississippi River valley and established numerous settlements. By the middle of the eighteenth century, France controlled more of the New World than any other European power, with control reaching from New Orleans up to the Great Lakes and northwest to modern-day Montana. However, between 1754 and 1763, France became embroiled in the French and Indian War and was forced to cede the Louisiana Territory to Spain in 1762. Spain did not have the resources to develop the territory, and had little involvement with the region during the next three decades.

Spain and France became allies against the British with the signing of the Second Treaty of San Ildefonso in 1796. Britain responded by using its navy to completely cut off Spain from North America. Napoleon, hoping to reestablish an empire in the region, took back control of Louisiana in 1800 when

Spain returned it as a result of the Third Treaty of San Ildefonso. This caused widespread concern within the United States that Napoleon would next attempt to forcibly take control of the Mississippi River and access to the Gulf of Mexico. However, continuing issues with colonial rebellions and an upcoming war with Britain forced him to abandon this plan.

Once America was invited to purchase the territory, negotiations for the land sale moved quickly. For the price of $15 million, the United States acquired 828,000 square miles (2,144,510 square kilomters) of land and doubled the size of the country overnight. In real terms, this deal meant that the land was purchased for roughly just three cents per acre. American expansion westward began immediately, and the following year a territorial government was established.

Even though interest was high, immediately following the purchase there was opposition and debate. Many in the House of Representatives opposed the acquisition and saw it as unconstitutional. They were concerned the United States had just handed over $15 million to start a war with Spain over ownership. The House attempted a vote to turn down the request for purchase, but it failed by just two votes. Some Federalists were concerned about how the country would be affected by the newly acquired western states, whose political and economic priorities would surely conflict with those of the bankers and merchants of New England. Others voiced concerns that an increase in slaveholding states in the new territory would worsen tensions between the Northern and Southern states. There was also opposition abroad as Spain denied the legitimacy of the transfer, claiming that France had previously promised not to sell Louisiana to a third party and that the transfer to French ownership had been contingent on having all European powers recognize their own king of Etruria. Since Britain refused to recognize this authority, Spain argued, the deal between Spain and France was void.

Modern historians have argued that the opposition of the New England Federalists was motivated more by economic self-interest than true concern over **constitutionality**. They were deeply anxious about western farmers gaining access to other avenues for transporting crops and no longer needing the use of New England ports. Many within the party bought and sold land outside their political group. Access to land out west would decrease the price and demand for their own properties. They were also worried that the western states would lean Democratic-Republican and thus could diminish the power of the Federalist Party within the House of Representatives.

two

The Young Sacagawea

"She was given the name Boo-wy-ee-puh, meaning 'Grass Woman,' perhaps to signify the summertime in which she was born."
— Rebecca Kay Jager

Traditionally, there has been very little concrete information on Sacagawea's early life. However, thanks to more modern historians who have thoroughly researched the culture and societies of different Native American tribes, it is now easier to build up a clearer picture of Sacagawea before she met Lewis, Clark, and the other members of the Corps of Discovery. Her younger years were characterized by constant movement and change, and Sacagawea learned quickly the importance of adjustment and adapting herself to new societies and cultures. These skills would serve her well in later life.

Opposite: Little is known about Sacagawea's early life.

Birth and Childhood: A Planned Life

Sacagawea is believed to have been born in either 1788 or 1789 to Shoshone parents living in what is now Idaho's Lemhi River valley. It is common among American Indians to receive more than one name during their lifetimes. When she was born, Sacagawea was given the name Boo-wy-ee-puh, meaning Grass Woman. This may have been a reference to a summertime birth. Later, she would be renamed Sacagawea, or Bird Woman, by the Hidatsa tribe, and in her final years she would sometimes be referred to as Lost Woman, Porivo (meaning "Chief"), and Water White-Man. It is generally believed that her father was a chief of the Shoshone tribe.

In accordance with Shoshone custom, shortly after she was born, Sacagawea was promised in marriage to an adult male of the Shoshone community. The standard payment for a marriage contract was horses. Like hundreds of Shoshone girls before her, Sacagawea was to remain with her parents while she completed her training in female tasks. Once she reached maturity, she would then be expected to join her intended and formally become his wife. The tribe's high demand for domestic labor during this period meant that Sacagawea grew up learning the necessary skills for numerous different kinds of skilled labor, as well as learning how to adapt to a harsh and nomadic lifestyle. If events had not conspired to alter the course of her life, she would most probably have followed the path set out for her by time and custom. However, when she was just twelve years old and mere months away from being finally delivered to her betrothed, Sacagawea was captured by Hidatsa warriors.

Capture and Life with the Hidatsa

While Sacagawea was still a child, her band was forced to move after surviving a severe smallpox outbreak. They retreated into the mountains toward the headwaters of the Missouri River, seeking protection. Much reduced in numbers, the Lemhi

Sacagawea's life with the Shoshones ended after her capture by Hidatsa warriors like this one.

Shoshones roamed the mountains for many years, surviving off edible plants.

In 1800, the Lemhi Shoshones was once again on the move. Sacagawea's father had called for a summer hunt, and the group intended to join the other Shoshone bands at the Three Forks of the Missouri River in present-day Montana. Without this hunt, the tribe would go hungry that winter. The band was traveling eastward across the Rockies. On the day of their departure, the group rose at dawn, and the women and girls packed away all of the belongings and shelters. For the next three days, Sacagawea walked alongside the procession as only men were allowed to ride on horseback.

Attacked

On the fourth day, while the band was encamped, they were suddenly attacked by a group of gun-bearing warriors from the Hidatsa tribe. This same group would later be referred to as the Minnetaree in documents by Lewis and Clark. Sacagawea would also later describe their attack to the explorers, who wrote in their journal about how the Shoshone braves, outnumbered and without guns, "mounted their horses and fled as soon as the attack began. The women and children, who had been berry-picking, dispersed, and Sacagawea, as she was crossing a shoal place, was overtaken in the middle of the river by her pursuers." In the heat of the attack, four men, four women, and a number of young boys were killed. Several girls and boys of the band were then captured and taken back to the Hidatsa village. The taking of captives was traditionally used to help replenish population loss in times of increased warfare and disease.

A New Life

The Hidatsas took Sacagawea and the other captives hundreds of miles east to their earth-lodge village along the Knife River, near present-day Bismarck, North Dakota. At the time, there were five Native American settlements in total within the area, two Hidatsa and three Mandan. Both tribes were involved in cross-cultural trade and had steady access to European goods. These came mainly through "free traders," independent European traders and trappers who sold to large fur trade companies. Prior to Sacagawea's capture, the Hidatsas had been involved in an intense period of war with the Lakota tribe. They had suffered huge losses and were now using the newly acquired peacetime to recover. Unlike the nomadic lifestyle Sacagawea had been raised in, Hidatsa culture was more technologically advanced and revolved around agriculture and farming.

The Hidatsa People: Society and Economy

The Hidatsas are a Siouan people, which means they are part of the Siouan language family of North America. Siouan dialects were generally spoken across the Great Plains, from Canada to Mississippi. The Hidatsa language is related to that of the Crows, and they are today considered to be a parent tribe of the modern Crow tribe in Montana. According to tribal tradition, the name "Hidatsa" derives from the word for "willow." The tribe was also referred to as the Minnetaree by their allies. For hundreds of years, the Knife River area in North Dakota was the home of both the Hidatsas and their ancestors. The very first Hidatsa villages date back all the way to the thirteenth century.

These Hidatsa villages were vital contributors to the plains trade network, where corn was the main **commodity**. Villages all along the Missouri River became a hub for indigenous commerce. Nomadic hunting groups would enter the valley in order to trade robes, meat, pelts, and eagle feathers in exchange for agricultural goods from the villagers. Women within these communities would trade agricultural products, including corn, along with domestic products. Men traded in horses, guns, and meat. Everyone within the plains trade network depended on corn as a vital source of nourishment. Within this environment, Sacagawea would grow into a teenager surrounded by diverse people who came to her new home to negotiate in a variety of languages.

The Hidatsas themselves lived in houses made of timber with earthen roofs. These gave far better protection than the animal skin tepees of the Lemhi Shoshones. Food was also more accessible and plentiful than Sacagawea had known before. The tribe cultivated a wide variety of native seeds and roots, wild vegetables and fruits, crops, and game. Even as a captive, Sacagawea's lifestyle became more comfortable, and she was not forced into a life of slavery. According to Hidatsa custom, after an initiation period, captives could be adopted as family members and join the community. Similar to the Shoshones, the Hidatsas practiced polygamy, and Sacagawea most likely became a wife of her male captor.

The Place of Hidatsa Women

By the standards of European society, Hidatsa women held a much higher social status than Shoshone women within their tribe. They fully participated in social and ceremonial organizations and played significant roles in religious rites and

Hidatsa women are believed to have held a more powerful position within their own tribe than the Shoshone women.

age-appropriate societies. Mothers negotiated the marriage of their daughters, but a daughter could resist her mother's choice if she objected to the groom. However, these marriages were still mainly formed for strategic purposes rather than for love. Also, as an adopted captive, it is probable that Sacagawea was not allowed these privileges.

The tribe community highly valued women's agricultural production and, in particular, their service to others. While living with the tribe, Sacagawea was educated in appropriate Hidatsa behavior for women and in female responsibilities. Hidatsa women were taught to care for the home in order to make others comfortable and happy, to be hospitable to strangers, and to be kind and helpful to neighbors, the needy, and the elderly. In particular, a woman was supposed to be dutiful to her husband, to be careful of his honor, and not to pursue other men. According to Rebecca Kay Jager, Hidatsa grandmothers passed the idea on to their daughters and granddaughters that a woman who "looked after her husband's comfort, guarded his interests, and showed hospitality to his guests would honor his name; he in turn would cherish her and they would be happy together."

Many European writers who met Sacagawea, or read records of her life, have since noted that she did indeed display many Hidatsa qualities. It was common for Europeans to recognize and project feminine traits onto Native women that were desirable to them, like submissiveness, domesticity, and physical attractiveness. However, any female characteristics or behaviors that they did not understand were often misinterpreted. For example, when Europeans saw the distribution of labor between tribal men and women, they were appalled. By European standards, Native women often were responsible for "men's work," such as raising crops, constructing homes, producing materials or products, and negotiating trades. They often depicted these women as beasts of burden in letters and books for European audiences back home.

One particular practice that was a serious point of contention between the two cultures was that of offering Native American women to outsiders as part of cross-cultural diplomacy. This practice had two purposes. First, women were believed to be good cultural **intermediaries**. The giving of women to an incoming group was thought to establish kinship and trust with foreigners. The women themselves would then be responsible for creating friendly relations between the two tribes and instructing the newcomers in Native standards of behavior. Second, women's nature and ability to give life was seen as a powerful transformative force. Her role was not just for procreation, but to transfer power and establish an alliance.

Incoming Europeans did not understand this philosophy as it contrasted so directly with their own beliefs about women and female chastity. They instead regarded the practice and the gendered division of labor as proof of savage immorality. Native women themselves were brought up to view this practice as service to their community within a society where female status depended on contributions and service to others. It is difficult to know exactly what women at this time thought about the practice. It is clear, however, in the cases of both Native American and European societies, that women were still treated as property. It was simply that the terms of their leases were approached from very different angles.

Sacagawea spent only a few years with the Hidatsa before she was herself given to a white man, the French Canadian fur trader Toussaint Charbonneau. The transaction was completed in order to ensure future cross-cultural interactions and trade. She may have simply been a useful woman, but her life experiences also made her a logical choice as a cross-cultural facilitator. She had grown up experiencing cultural dislocation and learned to adapt to new societies, and she would be able to teach Charbonneau about plains trade as well as the customs of the local villages. She was also skilled in languages. Though to modern standards this was not a pleasant prospect for a young woman, for Sacagawea the match offered her the opportunity to increase her own social status and influence among the tribe.

The Call of the West

At the time of Sacagawea's birth, European Americans had only recently arrived on the Northwest coast. While they knew of the Rocky Mountains, there had been little to no actual explorations of the area. In the late 1700s, the United States was still an extremely young country. It consisted of just thirteen loosely confederated states along the Atlantic, with no land west of the Mississippi. Native Americans in western North America had interacted on and off with Europeans for more than a century previous. Great Britain and France had been exploiting the region's resources since the early 1670s through the activities of the Hudson's Bay Company and the North West Company. The European Americans were the last foreigners to arrive, but their entrance would radically alter the political dynamic of the West.

Prior to the Corps of Discovery's expedition, there were many myths held by Americans about the West. Books, written by men who had never been to the region, described unicorns,

Many white settlers believed that moving west would provide them with greater freedom and wealth.

giant woolly mammoths, 7-foot-tall (2.1-meter-tall) beavers, and even blue-eyed, Welsh-speaking American Indians. Similarly, the land itself was described as consisting of erupting volcanoes and mountains of salt. The maps of the area were equally fantastical. Some European geographers even depicted California as an island. However, the most alluring of all the West's myths was a possibility of the "Northwest Passage."

Jefferson's Ambitions

The Northwest Passage was a hypothetical river, or sequence of rivers, that would cut across the mountains and eventually connect with the Pacific Ocean. If real, it would have provided a more direct route to Asia, enabling faster commerce. Finding

Charred Body and the Hidatsa People

The Hidatsa people were not one **homogenous** culture but in fact consisted of three large and distinct groups: the Awaxawis, the Awatixas, and the Hidatsa Proper.

The Awaxawis, or Amahamis, believed themselves to have first emerged from the earth at Devil's Lake in North Dakota. Prior to 1782, they had few enemies and had sufficient numbers to ward off attacks from enemy tribes. However, when they attempted to move upstream of the Knife River and establish a permanent settlement, they were driven out by the Hidatsa Proper, and war broke out between the two groups.

The creation myths of the Awatixas describe them descending from the sky led by the mythic Hidatsa folk hero Charred Body. Hidatsa folk traditions tell that Charred Body brought the Awatixa people to earth from their original home in the sky. However, he also

A Hidatsa warrior in traditional dance costume

introduced murder to the world by killing a woman who had insulted him. In Native American tradition, Charred Body is the uncle of the sacred twins Lodge-Boy and Thrown-Away. Charred Body is an important and heroic figure in Hidatsa mythology. He is believed to have populated the first Awatixa village and taught its people the Naxpike, or Hide-Beating Ceremony, and the Buffalo-Calling Ceremony. The first Awatixa people are believed to have lived near Painted Woods and then moved into the land between Heart River and Knife River along the Middle Missouri River.

The Hidatsa Proper, also known as the Hiratsas, were the largest of the three groups. They were in fact a league of numerous nomadic Hidatsa bands from the north, who settled in present-day Minnesota. During their travels, they met the Mandan tribe and then moved westward and settled alongside these new allies north of the Knife River. Later they would move right to the mouth of the Knife River, where they adopted agriculture and built permanent settlements.

the Northwest Passage had been a motivation of much North American exploration, and it was also the driving force behind the creation of the Corps of Discovery. Thomas Jefferson had long dreamed of American expansion across the continent. He was something of an armchair explorer. His personal library was filled with volumes on Portuguese, Spanish, and English excursions into the New World, and he was particularly interested in the northwestern fur trade. He first began planning to explore the land northwest of the Missouri River before he became president, and even before the United States had purchased the Louisiana Territory.

The Lewis and Clark Expedition

Prior to the Louisiana Purchase, Jefferson had secured initial funds from Congress for an expedition into the Louisiana Territory. Despite the dispute raging between France, Spain, and England over claims to the region, he was determined to

The Corps of Discovery traversed multiple rivers during their journey.

authorize a military **reconnaissance** of the area. He was wary of dissenters within the Federalist Party and so had phrased his request to emphasize the potential commercial benefits of the expedition. Jefferson also kept the financial request small, just $2,500, although the actual cost of the trip would later reach over $38,000. Furthermore, by this point in time he had hired Captain Meriwether Lewis of Virginia as his private secretary, ignoring more experienced candidates. In 1803, Jefferson named Lewis captain of the Corps of Discovery.

Lewis requested the help of Albert Gallatin to make a map of North America from the Pacific coast to the Mississippi. The lack of detail in maps from the period reveals the enormity of the task map collector Gallatin had before him. Gallatin was only able to produce a map with three points of certainty: the mouth of the Columbia River; the mouth of the St. Louis River; and rough aspects of the Missouri River up to the Mandan villages in modern-day Bismarck, North Dakota. It also illustrated how the Rocky Mountains might look and estimated the course of the Columbia, which had not been charted beyond its mouth. However, much of the map was left entirely blank. It was impossible for the European Americans to add further detail until someone traveled to the region, took measurements, and documented the geography of the land. Neither did the explorers know what plants, animals, and people to expect. Jefferson felt that the observation of commercial and agricultural possibilities of the territory was equally important to learning the terrain.

As soon as the Louisiana Purchase was finalized, Lewis left Washington, DC, for Pittsburgh to purchase provisions and hire an expedition crew. For Lewis, the purchase had transformed a secret mission through foreign land into a survey of American

Prior Expeditions

Before the Louisiana Purchase and the Lewis and Clark expedition, there were other European American explorers who pushed back the boundaries of their settlements. In 1775, Daniel Boone set out from Virginia under the employ of the Transylvania Company. This was a short-lived colony founded by land speculator and prominent North Carolina judge Richard Henderson. The company had hired Boone to establish a trail through what would later be known as the Cumberland Gap and into southeastern Kentucky. This trail was later named the Wilderness Road. Boone was an experienced hunter who had been traveling through southeastern Kentucky long before any settlements were founded. The journey was extremely dangerous and escalated tensions with local Native American tribes. Indeed, the party was attacked on several occasions—mostly likely by either Cherokee or Shawnee bands that had traditionally held the area as their tribal hunting grounds.

Boone traveled with a band of roughly thirty followers and marked a path to the Kentucky River, where he established Boonesborough. This was located close to modern-day Lexington, Kentucky. Despite the difficulties, Boone survived the journey there and back, and he later brought his family and other settlers to the newly established town in September 1775. He was closely followed by Henderson himself, who brought with him another expedition. They set about widening the path created by Boone in order to accommodate the wagons of later travelers. However, the Transylvania Company faced numerous difficulties in establishing its claim to the land, which had been previously claimed by both Virginia and North Carolina. When Henderson petitioned the newly formed Congress to make Transylvania a legally recognized colony, they declined, stating that they could not agree without the consent of both Virginia and North Carolina.

territory. Jefferson was equally excited by the prospect. He sent Lewis with a comprehensive document detailing specific instructions about the type of information to collect on the journey. He wanted to know more about the Natives: their languages, customs, and medicines. He requested details of flora and fauna, minerals, and significant geographical features. In particular, he asked for the party to explore the potential for trade opportunities.

Jefferson used every tool possible to ensure the success of the trip. He even gave Lewis a letter guaranteeing "the faith of the United States" to reimburse any party for goods or services Lewis deemed necessary for the expedition, essentially giving the captain a limitless line of credit. To Jefferson's mind, the expedition would not only chart the new territory of the United States but also determine its destiny.

three

The Corps of Discovery and Life Beyond

"The Intertrepeter & Squar [sic] who were before me at some distance danced for the joyful Sight, and She made signs to me that they were her nation."—William Clark

By the age of fourteen, Sacagawea was considered an adult within Native American society. It was at this time that she married Toussaint Charbonneau, a French Canadian trader living within the village. Charbonneau first arrived in the Knife River area in 1797. He was working as a

Opposite: Sacagawea's meeting and journey with the Corps of Discovery would add further adventures to her already tumultuous life.

free trader with connections to the North West Company. Upon arrival, he developed a rudimentary form of sign language and made both business and social connections with the Plains American Indians. This had been primarily achieved by the accepting of Native wives, a style of diplomacy that was common throughout indigenous America. Quickly realizing the "value" of multiple Native wives, Charbonneau took advantage of tribal customs of gender expectations. In addition to Sacagawea, he married another Shoshone Native woman known as Otter Woman.

Both Sacagawea and Otter Woman would have been responsible for domestic household labor and for the commercial labor associated with Charbonneau's trading practice. As previously discussed, Native-European marriages helped connect Europeans to Native American trade and facilitated communications between the two parties, as well as providing skilled labor to process hides from the hunt. While not a flattering prospect for any twenty-first-century woman, it was a key position in frontier society at the time. Native American societies supported such unions because they allowed the tribes to gain access to European goods and weapons, and to gain insider knowledge of the foreigners.

The Corps of Discovery

The Corps of Discovery was a specially designed unit of the United States Army. It formed the center of the Lewis and Clark expedition, a venture intended to map out the recently purchased Louisiana Territory. The outfit was led by Captain Meriwether Lewis and Second Lieutenant William Clark. The objectives of the mission were both commercial and scientific.

Jefferson wanted to learn more about the region and was interested in its resources and potential financial opportunities.

Lewis heralded from Virginia. Just two years prior to the expedition, he had been hired by Jefferson as a private secretary. His army experience included time with the First American Regiment, and he had served in both the Ohio Valley and the Northwest Territory. Following the expedition's completion, Lewis would later become governor of the Louisiana Territory.

Clark similarly hailed from Virginia. He had joined the army in 1792 and served in the Northwest Indian War. Four years later, he resigned from the army to return to his family's business. After accepting Lewis's offer to join the scheme, he was given a second lieutenant's commission instead a captain title due to the army's seniority system. However, this was not revealed to the rest of the Corps of Discovery, who referred to the lieutenant as "Captain Clark." After his return from the expedition, Clark went on to a political career that included the post of governor of the Missouri Territory.

The Corps also included a number of noncommissioned officers and privates, almost all of whom were experienced outdoorsmen and hunters.

Meeting Lewis and Clark

In the winter of 1804 through 1805, the Corps of Discovery arrived near the Hidatsa villages. Their intention was to build a base, gather knowledge and supplies, and pass the winter before continuing on their journey. Throughout the cold months, Lewis and Clark met with Native American leaders and European traders to gather information on the course of the river, the region's weather patterns, and the mountain

In some statues with Lewis and Clark, Sacagawea is portrayed as kneeling or almost cowering behind the explorers.

passes that lay to the west. They were also looking for a possible water route to the Pacific Ocean, and for any information on other First Nations peoples they might encounter. It was during this time that the two captains discovered that the Lemhi Shoshone Natives were considered the horse specialists of the northern Rockies.

Sacagawea was sixteen years old and pregnant with her first child when Lewis and Clark arrived in her village. She had been married to Charbonneau for roughly two years and had learned how to adapt to a multicultural environment and to the cultural differences between herself and her French husband. She was familiar with a broad stretch of the Northwest due to her travels with the Shoshones and capture by the Hidatsas, had developed a wide range of survival skills, and had mastered the ability to communicate on a **multilingual** frontier.

Native Perspectives and European American Intentions

To Native eyes, the Corps of Discovery's mission was a peculiar one. All previous invaders to the Great Plains had come in search of commodities, such as precious metals and furs. Jefferson's instructions to the group were to maintain tribal peace, spread American sovereignty, gather geographical and ethnological information, and inventory the region's resources. This was puzzling to the Native people, and Lewis and Clark had difficulty explaining their motives to the tribes whose paths they crossed.

The corps were particularly concerned with avoiding earning a reputation as greedy exploiters out for conquest and profit. However, the northwestern fur trade was a key concern. Aside from the financial possibilities of the fur trade, the alliances created by trade between Native American nations and the English and French traders were a threat to US sovereignty. Before arriving at the Hidatsa villages, a miscommunication between the corps and a band of Sioux Natives reinforced to the group the importance of building relationships with the different tribes and the severe need to communicate clearly with the indigenous people.

When the corps first met the Hidatsas, it was a culturally enlightening experience for both sides. As Rebecca Kay Jager describes, "These were unlike any other white men the Indians had met; they were explorers, ethnographers, and bureaucrats who represented a great father in the East. Village Indians, who were accustomed to outsiders and adept at cultural tolerance for the purpose of trade, were accommodating."

Preparation

That winter, Lewis and Clark interviewed a number of trappers who could possibly help to interpret with Natives and lead the expedition up the Missouri River the following spring. Eventually they decided to employ Charbonneau after discovering that he spoke passable Hidatsa and that his wife Sacagawea spoke Shoshone. Both captains were extremely aware that they would need the help of the Shoshone tribe for guidance and horses across the Rockies. According to their journals, neither Lewis nor Clark particularly liked Charbonneau; nevertheless, Sacagawea was considered so valuable and talented that Charbonneau was hired specifically for his wife's services. Significantly, Charbonneau was paid for their interpretation work, but not Sacagawea. One week later, the couple moved into Fort Mandan, and Clark nicknamed Sacagawea "Janey." The term "Jane" was a common slang word at the time for a woman.

On February 11, 1805, Sacagawea gave birth to her first child—a little boy. He was named Jean Baptiste. The rest of the Corps of Discovery nicknamed him "Little Pomp" or "Pompy," and he soon became beloved by the entire band. Only a month later, the expedition was experiencing problems. Charbonneau suddenly threatened to leave the trip, taking Sacagawea and their child with him. Some historians have argued that he could have been concerned over the effect of the harsh journey on his young family or that he was annoyed by the attention paid to Sacagawea by the rest of the band. Others have stated he was more likely trying to negotiate for better terms with the corps. He had realized the value of Sacagawea and wanted to use it to avoid the other responsibilities of joining the expedition, such as guard duty and restrictions on supplies.

Lewis and Clark were glad to be rid of Charbonneau, but were concerned over the loss of Sacagawea, who they knew would be extremely useful once they reached Shoshone territory. Charbonneau tried to wait the captains out, but after seeing preparations continue without him and no word of reconciliation, he wrote anxiously to Lewis and Clark asking to return. Just three weeks before the group's departure, Charbonneau was restored to the Corps on the proviso that Sacagawea would accompany the Corps.

Another member of the team was a Frenchman named George Drouillard, who specialized in Native American sign language. Lewis and Clark had hired Drouillard at the start of their trip in St. Louis. He was identified as the official translator for the expedition, though his skills were often inadequate. However, like Charbonneau, he was paid for his services. Sacagawea, acting as interpreter, guide, and cultural advisor, received no pay.

The Expedition

In April 1805, Sacagawea and the Corps of Discovery left Fort Mandan and journeyed up the Missouri River. They traveled in pirogues, small, flat-bottomed boats made for shallow water, which needed to be both poled and sometimes pulled from the riverbanks. They were very light and designed to tip over easily to get rid of water. The following month, the pirogues almost caused a severe loss for the team.

On May 14, one of the boats capsized, throwing weeks of research and specimens into the river. They would have been permanently lost were it not for the quick thinking of Sacagawea. She rescued many items from the water, including the journals of Lewis and Clark. The captains were impressed with her quick actions, and on May 20 they named the Sacagawea River in her honor. Lewis described her in his journal as "the Indian woman, to whom I ascribe equal fortitude and resolution, with any person onboard at the time of the accident," while simultaneously criticizing Charbonneau as "still crying to his god for mercy" and "perhaps the most timid waterman in the world."

As the journey entered its third month, Sacagawea became severely ill. Lewis chronicled her sickness in his journal:

> About 2 PM I reached the camp found the Indian woman extremely ill and much reduced by her indisposition. This gave me some concern, as well as for the poor object herself, then with a yung [sic] child in her arms, as from her condition of being our only dependence for a friendly negotiation with the Snake Indians, on whom we depend for horses to assist us in our portage from the Missouri to the Columbia River.

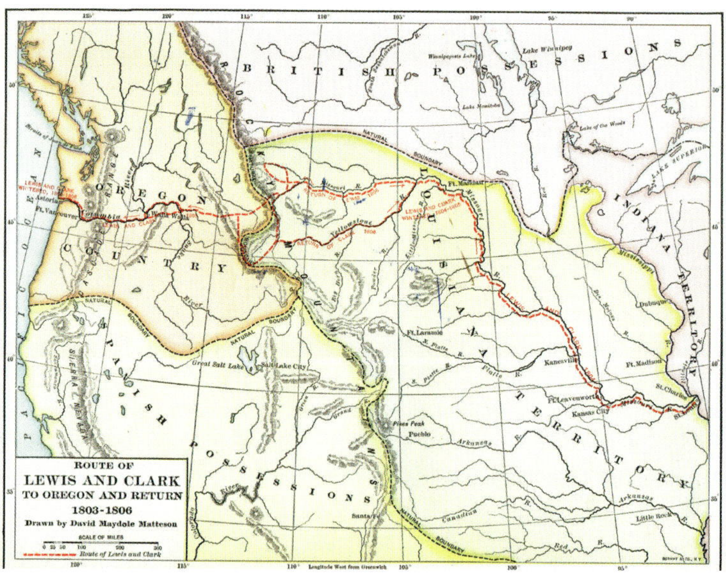

A Map of the route the Corps of Discovery traveled along the Missouri River

For the next ten days, her condition was carefully monitored and methodically recorded. When she eventually recovered, the entire band was hugely relieved. In the words of the scholar Rebecca Kay Jager, "Her sickness was the captains' foremost concern, and her recovery was a great relief."

As June moved into July, the corps entered the mountainous portion of their journey. It was at this juncture that finding the Shoshones became imperative. The group could see signs of Native Americans, but none could be found. It was then that Sacagawea began to recognize some of the landmarks of her homeland and was able to lead the group to where her people would likely be encamped. This was a cause for much celebrating among the corps as they had been traveling on foot, carrying their essentials, and by now the rocks and cacti had shredded the soles of their shoes.

Reunion

By August, Sacagawea had led the group into her homelands, and they discovered a Shoshone tribe. Lewis and Clark attempted to trade for horses to cross the Rocky Mountains. The chief was initially reluctant until the captains told him about the Shoshone woman who was traveling with them. They insisted the chief come and meet her. When the pair met, Sacagawea was overjoyed. The chief of the band was Cameahwait, her brother, whom she had not seen since her kidnapping by the Hidatsas. Lewis logged the reunion in his journal:

> Shortly after Capt. Clark arrived with the Interpreter Charbono, and the Indian woman, who proved to be a sister of the Chief Cameahwait. The meeting of those people was really affecting, particularly between Sah-cah-gar-we-ah and an Indian woman, who had been

> taken prisoner at the same time with her, and who had afterwards escaped from the Minnetarees and rejoined her nation.

Clark similarly noted the event in his journal: "The Intertrepeter & Squar [sic] who were before me at some distance danced for the joyful Sight, and She made signs to me that they were her nation."

After a proper reunion between Sacagawea and her people, negotiations continued, but this time with more goodwill. The Shoshones agreed to exchange for horses and to provide guides to lead the Corps of Discovery over the treacherous Rocky Mountains.

The Rockies

From August to November, the band trekked the Rockies. It was a grueling journey, and at points they were forced to eat tallow candles, made from fat, in order to survive. When they finally emerged on the other side and descended into the warmer climate, they regained their strength thanks to Sacagawea's knowledge of edible plants.

As the company reached the Pacific Coast and the mouth of the Columbia River, Sacagawea showed herself to be hugely generous as well as an invaluable cultural intermediary. She offered her own beaded belt to allow the captains to barter for a fur robe that they wanted as a gift for President Jefferson. The event was recorded in Clark's diary, though it seems rather lacking in appreciation for Sacagawea's generosity:

> One of the Indians had on a roab made of 2 Sea Otter Skins the fur of them were more butifull than any fur I had ever Seen both Capt. Lewis & my Self endeavored to purchase the roab with different articles at length we

precured it for a belt of blue beeds which the Squar-wife of our interpreter Shabono [Charbonneau] wore around her waste [sic]."

In November, the team finally arrived at the Pacific Ocean, and all members of the outfit, including Clark's black slave York, voted on the location for erecting their winter fort. Sacagawea advised the group to pick a spot where they would find plenty of potatoes, but she was outvoted. It was after this that the corps built Fort Clatsop.

A few months later, in January, a dead whale washed up onto the beach south of the fort. Clark planned to take a small group to the beach to gather fat and other resources from the carcass, leaving behind much of the crew, including Sacagawea. Sacagawea, however, would have none of this. Describing her frustration, Clark later wrote, "[She] was very

The journey across the Rocky Mountains would prove to be one of the toughest portions of the entire expedition.

The American Frontier

Exploring and expanding the Western United States has been a long and complex journey. Traditionally this area was called the American Frontier, and though it now conjures images of cowboys, deserts, and unrestricted freedom, it was still largely unknown when westward exploration began in the early seventeenth century with the arrival of English colonialists. Typically, the American Frontier refers to land west of the Mississippi River, whereas initial European American settlements were focused largely in the East.

Prior to 1776, the West was a focus for both settlers and politicians of different nationalities. English, French, Spanish, and Dutch immigrants all arrived on the shores of the Americas looking for opportunities to live a better life than they had left behind. A few thousand French settlers migrated to Canada and established communities along the St. Lawrence River. French fur traders traveled throughout the Great Lakes and the Miwest, but they rarely settled down for long. Within the United States itself, French exploration was confined to a few very small villages, such as Kaskaskia in Illinois, and New Orleans. Dutch settlers set up fur trading posts in the Hudson River valley. These were quickly followed by large grants of land to rich landowning gentlemen, who brought in tenant farmers to create compact, permanent villages. This created heavy rural settlement in upstate New York but did not push toward westward expansion.

Gradually the influx of different nations into the United States began to create something uniquely American—the frontiersman. Recognized today by their clothing, frontiersmen had to be able to survive any conditions and learn any skill. This was reflected in their leather trousers, moccasins, fur cap, hunting shirt, and often a belt with a hunting knife and shot pouch—all homemade. The frontiersmen lived in rough lean-to houses or at most a one-room shack.

impatient to be permitted to go with me … She observed that She had traveled a long way with us to See the great waters, and that now that monstrous fish was also to be Seen, She thought it very hard that She could not be permitted to See either (She had never yet been to the [ocean])." As a result, Sacagawea joined the team heading to the beach and saw not only her "monstrous fish" but also the ocean for the first time in her life.

Finding the Ocean and the Journey Home

As the spring of 1806 rolled around, the company prepared to leave Fort Clatsop and head back east. After months of trekking, they arrived back at the Rocky Mountains in July 1806. This was not just a simple return journey, and Sacagawea's skills were still necessary in order for Lewis and Clark to gather information. The band was attempting to figure out a quicker and safer way through the mountains when Sacagawea spoke up. She told Clark that she had been to this plain frequently during her time with the Shoshones and knew of a gap between the mountains that would allow for easier passage. This "gap" would later become known as the Gibbons Pass. A week later, her geographical knowledge would prove itself again when she advised Lewis and Clark to cross back through the Yellowstone Basin. The route proved so useful that later it was chosen as the best path for the Northern Pacific Railway to traverse the continental divide. Today it is known as the Bozeman Pass.

In August, the group finally reached Fort Mandan once again. There was an emotional farewell before the corps, minus Sacagawea and her family, left for home. For his services, Charbonneau was paid $500.33. Sacagawea received nothing.

Aftermath

As the Corps of Discovery traveled homeward down the river from Fort Mandan, Clark began almost instantly to miss the little Jean Baptiste, and he composed a letter to Charbonneau:

> You have been a long time with me and conducted your Self in Such a manner as to gain my friendship, your woman who accompanied you that long dangerous and fatigueing rout to the Pacific Ocian and back diserved a greater reward for her attention and services on that rout than we had in our power to give her at the Mandans. As to your little Son (my boy Pomp) you well know my fondness of him and my anxiety to take him and raise him as my own child … If you are desposed to accept either of my offers to you and will bring down you Son your famn [femme,

> woman] Janey had best come along with you to take care of the boy untill I get him … Wishing you and your family great success & with anxious expectations of seeing my little danceing boy Baptiest I shall remain your Friend, William Clark.

He clearly had developed a strong emotional connection to Jean Baptiste, perhaps severely feeling the lack of his own family while on the journey. However, some historians have argued that in fact Charbonneau was a violent man and that Clark had feared for the child's safety. Though nothing would come of this request straightaway, Clark's offer was noted by the family and stayed fixed in their minds.

The trip became an overnight sensation thanks to the American press. Its success gave Jefferson a huge political victory and turned Lewis and Clark into heroes. Their journals were edited and published soon after. Scholars and historians took the story under their wing to compose further records of the birth of the American nation. None wrote about Sacagawea, not for almost one hundred years.

Many historians have debated Sacagawea's role within the Corps of Discovery. Exactly how useful was she as a guide? Was her role exaggerated? These questions are further complicated by more modern interpretations of her as someone who helped the very nation that had purchased her own people's land right out from beneath their feet. However, these concerns both minimize her abilities and exaggerate her effect. Sacagawea was not attempting to act as a political figure. She was surviving within a society where life was difficult and often short. She was an extremely strong and brave woman, whose knowledge of the region was extensive, and her presence as an ambassador of peace helped to avoid unnecessary conflict and bloodshed.

Gender Roles and Equality

In early encounters between European and Native American communities, European men were particularly confused and even horrified by the work undertaken by Native American women. This work was often tiring and labor intensive, including tasks like farming in addition to traditional childcare. To the European mind, these women were being treated like pack mules and acted only as further proof of Native inferiority. This narrow-minded reasoning failed to take into account Native American perceptions of gender work balance which worked along principles of reciprocity, balance, and autonomy. In fact, most historians agree that at the time of contact, Native American women actually had more authority and autonomy than European women.

First Nations societies were generally run within a system where mutual obligation and respect bound people as much as kinship, extended family, and clan did. Concepts of reciprocity were used to determine work allocation between the sexes. Men were generally responsible for hunting, warfare, and interacting with outsiders. Women managed internal operations within a community. They owned the family's housing and personal goods, produced food, and reared children. These activities were held in high esteem within Native communities, and so women held important political, social, and economic power. In many Native American tribes, membership and material goods were passed down the female line. In these matrilineal societies, clan matrons selected men to serve as their chiefs, and they had the power to depose a chief who had proved himself unworthy.

Their roles as life givers seeped into Native American mythology. In many creation stories, it is women who create life on earth or who use their bodies to create the earth itself.

It cannot be said exactly where her political alliances fell as we have no written documents by her. However, she cannot be held responsible for the entirety of relations between the United States and Native Americans thereafter.

This memorial at the Wind River Reservation in Wyoming remains a controversial spot as opinion is divided over whether it is indeed Sacagawea's final resting place.

Later Life and Death

Sacagawea and her husband spent three more years living among the Hidatsas, and in 1809 they eventually accepted Clark's invitation to join him and settle in St. Louis, Missouri. Charbonneau took possession of the 320 acres (130 hectares) of land in St. Louis he earned for his services to the Corps of Discovery. They also entrusted the care of their son, Jean Baptiste, to Clark, who enrolled the young boy into the Saint Louis Academy Boarding School. Roughly a year later, Sacagawea gave birth to a daughter, whom she named Lizette.

By 1811, the couple had moved to Fort Manuel Lisa on the Missouri River. Fully adjusted to the frontier life, Charbonneau could not adjust to a more settled and comfortable existence in St. Louis. He sold his property to Clark for just $100 before uprooting Sacagawea and their daughter and moving to the fort. Their son was left with Clark. However, a year after the move, Sacagawea became gravely ill. Henry Brackenridge, a fur dealer at the fort's trading post, noted that Sacagawea "had become sickly and longed to revisit her native country." Whether her homesickness was exacerbated by her illness or vice versa, she was not in a condition to travel.

The following year, in December 1812, Sacagawea died. A clerk named John Luttig, also living at Fort Manuel Lisa, recorded the event in his journal, stating that she "died of putrid fever," most likely **typhus**, only twenty-five years old. Only months later, Fort Manuel Lisa was attacked by a Native band, and fifteen inhabitants were killed. Sacagawea's daughter Lizette and the clerk John Luttig were among the survivors. Almost immediately, Clark became the formal guardian of both Lizette and Jean Baptiste. It is believed Lizette did not survive past infancy. History is hazy over Charbonneau's whereabouts at this point. Some have stated that Charbonneau was not in the fort when Sacagawea died and had still not returned by the time of the attack, while others have argued that he was in fact killed during the assault on Fort Manuel Lisa.

Despite this sad ending, there are other stories that Sacagawea did not die at Fort Manuel Lisa on the Missouri River. Some Native American oral traditions say instead that she left her husband and crossed back over the plains. By leaving her husband's "band," under Shoshone custom, their marriage was considered dissolved, and Sacagawea remarried into a Comanche tribe. It is also stated that later, in 1860, she eventually returned to the Shoshones in Wyoming, where she died in 1884. Evidence for this version of events is thin. However, there are records of a Shoshone woman, bearing Sacagawea's name and telling stories about leading foreigners over the plains, who died in Wyoming. Despite these stories, most historians believe that she did indeed die in 1812.

four

Native American Women and the Wild West

***"When you go looking for missing persons, you may not find them, but you are bound to find out a lot of other things."*—Virginia Scharff**

Scharff's words cut to the heart of the Sacagawea story. The mythology surrounding her often not only misinterprets the accomplishments of a real Shoshone woman but also ignores the help and guidance of many other First Nations women. As has been previously stated, finding the true face of Sacagawea is a difficult task. We have no idea what she looked like, and historians still continue to argue

Opposite: The American West is commonly known for wide-open plains and an arid climate.

over how to spell her name correctly. As such, it is tempting to **romanticize** her or build information into her biography that we could not possibly know, never mind have concrete proof of. Some scholars have mistakenly portrayed her as a metaphorical midwife to the American West or have written off her contributions entirely. These are both equally wrong.

Accomplishments

Sacagawea's achievements were not just her geographical knowledge or her linguistic capabilities, but also her day-to-day activities that helped ensure the survival of the Corps of Discovery—the domestic tasks she was responsible for, the food she gathered even in the difficult terrain of the Rocky Mountains, and so forth. What is equally obvious is that her story is but the tip of the iceberg. Many Native Americans helped guarantee the success of the Lewis and Clark expedition, and while many of the men were named in the captains' journals, the women almost never were. Their contributions have become erased and unknown. To fully understand Sacagawea's achievements, it is important to look at her successes and challenges, and equally important to examine the overlooked contributions of other Native American women to the expedition.

Cross-Cultural Communication

Throughout her short life, Sacagawea divided her time between Shoshone, Hidatsa, French Canadian, and American cultures. This placed her in a unique position to understand and interpret connections and similarities. Her facilitation helped these extremely different groups not only to understand each other but also to work together for a common cause.

Her key tasks involved recognizing landmarks to aid navigation, carrying messages between the captains, and taking part frequently in the long and complex process of translating conversations among the European Americans and the various Native American tribes they encountered. During such talks, Sacagawea, Charbonneau, and the Frenchman Drouillard would form a translation chain, with Sacagawea converting the spoken language into Hidatsa, Charbonneau converting Hidatsa into French, and then Drouillard relaying this into English for Lewis and Clark. It involved clear communication and concentration, and was vital in establishing friendly relations with tribes in order to secure resources, guidance, and safe passage across the territory.

Sacagawea's abilities gave her a good reputation among the men of the Corps of Discovery, in particular Clark. He clearly liked and respected the young Shoshone woman and had seen for himself her bravery, resourcefulness, and adventurous nature on many occasions. The feeling was mutual. On Christmas Day 1805, Sacagawea presented Clark with ten white weasel tails as a gift of appreciation. Later, after leaving Charbonneau, Sacagawea, and Jean Baptiste at Fort Mandan on their return journey home, Clark wrote a letter to Charbonneau claiming, "Your woman who accompanied you that long dangerous and fatiguing rout to the Pacific Ocian and back diserved a greater reward for her attention and services on that rout than we had in our power to give her at the Mandans." Though Lewis and Clark displayed a somewhat **condescending** attitude to Sacagawea in their journals, here Clark did at least acknowledge the service she had given them.

Survival Skills

It is arguable that, in many ways, Sacagawea had been training for the Lewis and Clark expedition for most of her life. She was born into a culture that knew how difficult nomadic life could be and how important it was to be able to survive

Sacagawea's ability to forage edible roots kept the expedition alive through harsh winters and hostile landscapes.

in a variety of weathers and terrains. As a Shoshone girl, she was educated at an early age in foraging and gathering foods. She was able to find edible roots and plants in harsh conditions, she was skilled in repairing and creating clothes and tools, and she knew how to pack and store goods for a large nomadic community. All these elements would prove useful on her journey. On many occasions, her knowledge of roots and plants kept the men alive with ingredients that the corps had never seen before, much less knew were edible. All this was in addition to her quick removal from Fort Mandan after a difficult labor, caring for a young infant, and doing the washing and other domestic tasks for the thirty-two men of the corps.

Capabilities of Women

Though her achievements would not be acknowledged for many years, Sacagawea was a strong example on the American Frontier of the physical and mental capabilities of women. Most of the white European Americans she traveled with were far more used to the company of white Western women, whose behavior was strictly controlled by society and their families and who were frequently characterized as weak and emotional creatures unequal to men's strength and logic. The unique opportunity of the expedition gave Sacagawea the chance to peel away some of the expectations of both her tribe and white explorers. Time and again she proved her physical toughness, her adaptability, and her critical thinking. As Virginia Scharff argues, "Her knowledge of the requirements of travel, her eagerness to journey to Shoshone territory, and her confidence in her own experience and skill in getting around the country the corps was about to 'discover' at least matched those of the expedition's men."

While she may not have been the corp's lead navigator by any stretch, without her guidance and knowledge it is highly likely that the journey would not have been completed. Further, without Sacagawea it is probable that the company would have been attacked by hostile tribes who believed the expedition to be a war party.

Challenges

Surprisingly, neither Lewis nor Clark expressed any concerns about exposing a new mother and her child to the grueling expedition that lay ahead. Despite the lack of credit paid to her in their journals, she was so crucial to their negotiations with the Shoshone tribe that they could not afford to lose her skills. When Sacagawea became sick some months into the journey, it is interesting that while Lewis does note concern for her welfare, he was more concerned by the prospect of losing their only Shoshone translator. Another likely reason for their lack of concern was the general view held by European Americans that indigenous women were closer to mules than women and thus were able to endure harsher burdens than their white counterparts. Interestingly, those who would later set out from the eastern United States to settle in the West would also heavily rely on women's ability to travel and work without making allowances for the challenges of sickness and childbirth.

Childbirth

Sacagawea first joined the expedition as a heavily pregnant teenager, and she was surely aware that she would be

In the nineteenth century, many Europeans believed that Native American women did not experience the pain of childbirth as much as European women.

undergoing the journey carrying and caring for a very small and vulnerable infant. When she finally did give birth at Fort Mandan in February 1805, those keeping diaries within the corps all noted her long and agonizing labor. Typically the birth of a first child is a difficult experience for any woman, and Sacagawea's labor was particular long and without the benefits of modern medicine. Lewis later noted that the only medicine she received was a drink containing the crushed rattles of rattlesnakes. This drink was believed by Native Americans at the time to help speed the birth.

Lewis and Clark were not the first European settlers to become convinced that Native American women gave birth with greater ease than Western women. Many accounts from early settlers described witnessing births where the expectant mother separated herself from the group, went to some solitary location, had her child without much pain, and got straight back on the road. Given that the majority of white men of this period did not even attend the labors of their own wives, it is difficult to believe that these accounts are entirely accurate. Research into this subject actually produces a very different picture.

While there were many different birth rituals practiced among First Nations peoples, there were some commonalities. In many tribes, a new birth was attended by close family members and select members of the wider community. During pregnancy, women paid special attention to their diet and activity in order to avoid harming the child. For example, some believed that eating raccoon or pheasant while pregnant could make the baby ill or even cause death. Many women engaged in rituals to guarantee a safe birth, such as a daily washing of the hands and feet, or the employment of a medicine man to help ease delivery.

Despite the various stories of solitary births, the majority of Native American women were attended by midwives and other close family. During delivery, the woman would stand, kneel, or sit, but she would never lie down. This was due to a belief that if a woman tried to give birth lying down, the baby

The Lewis and Clark expedition used "pirogues," or canoes, to navigate up the Missouri River and carry their equipment.

would never come out. While European descriptions of Native American women's lightning-fast recovery are undoubtedly exaggerated, their excellent physical conditioning certainly helped in their recovery time. Barring serious complications, often First Nations women were able to return to their daily lives in a very short amount of time.

The Demands of the Journey

In Sacagawea's Nickname: Essays on the American West, writer Larry McMurtry describes in detail the hardships that Sacagawea would have faced on her westward trip:

> For a young woman to travel cross the upper West at the beginning of the nineteenth century with thirty-two men and a baby was no bed of roses. Her nautically challenged husband twice nearly dumped her and the baby accidentally into the icy Missouri River. Because of her infant she and her husband slept in the captain's tent, a proximity that may not always have been easy. In June of 1805 she got seriously ill—Captain Lewis, who carefully nursed her back to health, suspected some blockage of the menses: she suffered all this while managing a young child and a cranky husband.

Over the course of the expedition, fifty-nine people and one dog, Lewis's Newfoundland named Seaman, participated in or aided the Corps of Discovery. However, only thirty-three people (and one dog) started at Fort Mandan and completed the entire journey. This was the central exploring party. It consisted of a core group of military men, contract boatmen or hunters, Clark's African American slave York, Sacagawea, her child, her husband, and George Drouillard. The other twenty-six volunteers were Native American men and women who joined the party for short periods to help guide, navigate, or transport baggage over particularly difficult or unfamiliar territory.

The route from Lewis and Clark's starting point in St. Louis all the way to the Pacific Ocean was roughly 3,700 miles (5,955 kilometers). Combined with the return journey back the trip was closer to 7,690 miles (12,376 km) and it took the Corps of Discovery two years, four months, and ten days to complete. Most historians believe that the party would only have been able to travel up to 14 miles (22.5 km) per day under good conditions. Life on the expedition was rough and hugely physically demanding. The group lived outdoors, hunted for food, and rowed their keelboat along the Missouri River, often having to tow the craft when the current became too strong or the river too difficult to navigate.

The expedition itself was a complex affair with both a large number of resources to be moved and cared for, and the constant threat of illness and injury. In total, the group's supplies were worth over $2,000 dollars—a huge amount of money for the time. They traveled with three boats, one 55-foot (17-meter) keelboat and two smaller canoe-like pirogues; two horses; thirty-five oars; and a broad sail. Every member traveled on foot with their own camping supplies and mapping equipment.

In addition, the members brought with them goods to trade with any Native American tribes they encountered, such as ivory combs, pocket mirrors, tobacco, hollowed-out tomahawks that doubled as pipes, thread, bright cloth, scissors, beads, and silk ribbons. Lastly, each member carried a small variety of medicines like quinine, opium, and mercury.

Health care was a very real problem on the journey. Sacagawea herself fell ill and was close to death during June 1805, and almost every member became ill at some point of the journey. Yet it was not just disease that the corps had to be cautious of. The route itself was difficult, and the travelers could be just as easily injured by a dangerous fall as by infection. Cold winters and long rains sapped their physical strength and tested their courage. Unfamiliar conditions often caused small injuries that sapped morale, such as the frequent foot injuries from prickly pear cacti. There were a number of boating accidents, falls from wet and rugged terrain, and simple slips with axes and knives. Though almost every member of the corps was injured during the trip, luckily none was hurt so badly as to need to return home. This was not the only part of nature that the group learned to contend with. As well as navigating unfamiliar and difficult terrain, the corps documented many encounters with mountain lions, coyotes, snakes, bobcats, foxes, and bears. In fact, it was on this trip that Clark saw his first ever grizzly bear.

In addition to the physical demands of the journey, there were many psychological ones. Its grueling nature meant that there could be no "passengers," and everyone had to pull his or her own weight, with the obvious exception of the baby Jean Baptiste. Every member, Sacagawea included, had to play his or her part in the mission and mentally give everything toward achieving the mission's goals. Without the willpower and drive of each individual, the expedition could not have succeeded. Sacagawea's mental toughness to survive each day and keep her son alive was at least equal to any male member of the team.

Between Cultures

Sacagawea was arguably a member of several cultures and none at the same time. Her frequent shifting between different Native American tribes and white European societies meant that she continually had to readjust her behavior and identity. It is likely that this would have caused some emotional anguish and confusion. Writer Carolyn Gilman notes, "[Her] experiences may have made her one of those people permanently stuck between cultures, not entirely welcome in her new life nor able to return to her old."

Sacagawea was taken from her own culture as a girl, was held captive among the Hidatsas, was one of two wives to a French Canadian husband, and spent her later life among white colonizers. It is therefore difficult to know where Sacagawea would truly have felt at home. However, it is notable that before her death in 1812, she was described in the diary of a Fort Manuel Lisa fur dealer as "a good creature, of a mild and gentle disposition … greatly attached to the whites, whose manners and airs she tries to imitate." The diary entry adds, however, that she was "long[ing] to revisit her native country," though it is unclear which native country was meant. In this description, it is not hard to see a woman trapped between cultures, not fully comfortable in either.

Contemporary Reactions

Native American women are largely an unsung element of the Lewis and Clark expedition. Their work and contributions have been traditionally downgraded and erased from contemporary accounts. Lewis and Clark are not exceptional in this regard. Many exploration accounts of the discovery and expansion of America fail to name First Nations women beyond Sacagawea or Pocahontas. More often than not, their presence is forgotten,

Native American Maps

The Native Americans held very different mapping traditions to Lewis and Clark. Unlike those of the European American captains, these maps were not concerned with the precise measuring of physical space. Rather, they were based on how much time it would take to travel, what might happen along the way, and what was important to remember about the places involved. Such maps often told narratives that reflected the location's connection with the seasons of the year and different events. Some even told the histories of different nations.

Native American maps reflect the concerns and priorities of Native travelers.

Lewis and Clark did not fully understand the premise of Native American maps. They were primarily interested in the physical design, rather than the conceptual. Their desire for knowledge of the land's physical attributes often blinded them to the significance of the land to First Nations peoples. This was partly because the two captains had very different intentions for their maps than the Native tribes they met. Lewis and Clark were primarily looking to create something that could be used by the American government and future settlers and traders.

In contrast, Native Americans did not need such permanent and precise information. Often maps were carved into hillsides or written in sand, and once the information was imparted, the map would be left to dissolve. If something more permanent was required, a charcoal sketch on animal skins was deemed sufficient. Native American maps also were not confined to a grid format, and different lines could look similar but in fact indicate rivers, trails, or war routes. In addition, such maps did not always orientate with north at the top but rather were organized by sunrise and sunset in line with the origin and final destination of the traveler.

or they are regulated to generic titles such as "a squaw" (now considered an offensive term) or "the Indian woman." Nonetheless, their quieter but often crucial contributions have been essential to the success of many missions, including the Lewis and Clark expedition.

Perceptions of Native American Women

As previously discussed, Lewis and Clark both believed that heavy physical labor performed by women marked a society as "savage" and thus in need of enlightenment and conquest. The division of labor between men and women in many Native American tribes was used by white settlers as proof of the justice of their colonialism. Yet even Lewis admitted in one diary entry that Shoshone women were "held more Sacred among them than in any nation we have seen and appear to have an equal Shere in all Conversation," a position not enjoyed by white European American women of the period.

However, despite their criticism of the physical labor relegated to Native American women, both Lewis and Clark were happy to benefit from Native women's strength and skill when needed. In fact, Shoshone women were employed to drive packhorses and cart excess baggage for the corps across the Continental Divide.

One particular moment of this passage struck Lewis forcefully with the strength of Shoshone women. During the journey, a Shoshone woman stopped by a stream and sent her two heavily loaded horses onward with the other women in the group. When Lewis asked Sacagawea's brother, Chief Cameahwait, what had delayed her, Cameahwait explained that the woman had stopped to give birth and would soon overtake the group. This she soon did. Lewis was shocked and confused by the new mother's strength and mobility, unable to match it with his preconceived ideas of womanhood. Forgetting his own experience of Sacagawea's painful and prolonged labor, he chalked the experience up to the entire Native American race's difference to white European Americans, stating, "It appears to me that the facility and ease with which the women of the aborigines of North America bring forth their children is rather a gift of nature than depending as some have supposed on the habitude of carrying heavy burdens on their backs while in a state of pregnancy." Whether or not this retelling of the event was accurate, with this statement, Lewis reduced one woman's achievement of human physical conditioning to a subject of study for the "enlightened" white explorer. He never even mentions her name. The episode further illustrates the mythology around Native American women compared to European American women.

As was typical for the period, the journals and writings of European Americans paid far more attention to indigenous men than women. Often, Native American men's names were documented, but only one woman's name, other than Sacagawea's, ever appears in the Lewis and Clark expedition journals. Watkuweis was an elder member of the Nez Percé tribe. Her band encountered Lewis and Clark on their travels, and in many ways her life was very similar to Sacagawea's. Translated into English, her name means "returned from far country." Long before her meeting with the Corps of Discovery, Watkuweis was captured by either a Blackfeet or Atsinas band, taken to Canada, and sold to a white trader. She lived in Canada for several years before finding her way home to the Nez Percé people.

According to the tribe's oral tradition, while the Corps of Discovery was staying in the village, most became severely ill with dysentery. The majority of the tribe was in favor of killing the explorers in their weakened state and taking their weapons and goods. Watkuweis, who held a positive view of whites from her time in Canada, dissuaded the men of her band and instead convinced them to assist the corps. However, despite this crucial help, Clark would later entirely erase her memory by omitting her name from his second, revised edition of his published journals.

Other women obscured by Lewis and Clark's journals include Sacagawea's childhood friend who was also captured as a child in the Hidatsa attack. When the corps met with the Shoshone people, Sacagawea was reunited not only with her brother but also with her longest friend. Lewis described the meeting in his diary:

> Capt. Clark arrived with the Interpreter Charbono, and the Indian woman, who proved to be a sister of the chief Cameah-wait. The meeting of these people was really affecting, particularly between Sah cah-gar-we-ah and an Indian woman, who had been taken prisoner at the same time with her, and who had afterwards escaped from the Minnetares and rejoined her nation.

This "Indian woman" is once again left unnamed. However, in this instance the omission seems especially surprising as, by Lewis's own admission, she had achieved alone what an army regiment of thirty-two men had required numerous guides, translators, and provisions to accomplish. In the words of scholar Virginia Scharff:

What Lewis failed to acknowledge was that, for a period spanning five arduous months, the Lewis and Clark expedition simply retraced the footsteps of this unnamed Shoshone girl, who years before, as a ten- or eleven- or twelve-year-old, had been taken captive and forced to travel the long road eastwards, then seen her chance to escape and, leaving her cherished friend behind, made the journey from the Mandan villages back to her people, on her own. Like Ginger Rogers dancing in high heels with Fred Astaire, this girl did what Lewis and Clark would, but under pressure, and backwards.

Lack of Information

The last major challenge Sacagawea has faced is a lack of written information on her life. Very few of the expedition's diarists wrote about her, and none thought to draw her. Historian Larry McMurtry points out that Lewis, in his journals, is mostly neutral about his Shoshone interpreter and even somewhat condescending, suggesting at one point that it would take only a few trinkets to make her happy. In particular, McMurtry notes the strangeness of Lewis's decision not to sketch her, saying, "[Lewis] drew an excellent fish, and the head of a gull, but left no image of the woman he traveled with for thousands of miles." Even Clark, who more clearly displayed a friendship with Sacagawea, wrote of their farewell at Fort Mandan and did not use her name, describing her simply as Charbonneau's "Snake Indian wife." This rather sad omission makes it hard for historians and scholars to fully understand Sacagawea's

A Fair Ending

One of the most popular myths of Sacagawea has been, interestingly, how and when she died. Most historical evidence points to her dying aged just twenty-five at Fort Manuel Lisa after a long battle with putrid fever. This understandably feels like a sad and unjust ending for such a young and brave woman. Many who have held her up as a feminist icon have also been dismayed by certain elements of her background.

According to written reports, Sacagawea's husband, Charbonneau, was not only twice her age but also a drunk who was known to beat his wives. There has been speculation that Clark's wish to adopt Sacagawea's son, Jean Baptiste, was motivated largely by a fear for the child's safety. Sacagawea never left this abusive relationship but instead died still married to Charbonneau, after handing over care of her son to Clark. Naturally, it is painful for modern audiences to contemplate such an early death after an equally harsh and violent life. It is therefore not surprising that the public would instead cling to the idea that Sacagawea left her abusive husband to travel back to her people, remarried, and died happily after a long and peaceful life in Wyoming. Though some Indian traditions do support this theory, there is very little evidence for it. Sadly, it is more likely the wishful thinking of a public mourning a figure owed a debt of gratitude that can never be repaid.

thoughts and feelings on the trip. Instead, they must be content with the few morsels dropped from the pens of Lewis and Clark.

Her Legend Lives On

Sacagawea was not a romantic Native princess, nor was she a passive observer. She was a human being placed in an extraordinary situation who made the best of her skills to survive and to protect her child. She was strong and capable, and a true asset to the Corps of Discovery. However, her contribution was largely underappreciated by the team, and often her strength was put down to racial differences rather than personal character. Her efforts stand as an example of the accomplishments of many Native American women who today have sadly been lost to history. Sacagaea's story did not end with her death. The world was soon to discover just how politically powerful her memory could be.

LIBERTY
IN GOD
VE TRUST
200
D

five

Sacagawea's Memory and the Modern World

"She is no hand-maiden to white ambition; she is the earth itself."
— Brian Dippie

Although complex and opaque, Sacagawea's story still plays an important part in US history. From the early twentieth century up to today, her image has been used in many different ways. She became a symbol of the expansion of America, an inspirational figure of the women's suffrage movement, and a celebration of Native American culture. Yet it is impossible to forget that Sacagawea was also misrepresented and reinterpreted in order to promote white narratives, and often the unique culture of her tribe and of other

Opposite: The Sacagawea Dollar was commissioned in 2000 and used a Shoshone model as there are no contemporary images of Sacagawea.

Native Americans was lost in the swirl of conflicting ideologies. This can be seen most clearly through an exploration of her modern-day recognition, her legacy, and the current status of Native American women's contributions to history.

Modern Recognition

Sacagawea has received recognition and awards from a number of organizations. As her story gained popularity in the early twentieth century, Sacagaewa was adopted by the National American Woman Suffrage Association as a symbol of women's worth and independence. They raised funds to erect several statues and plaques in her memory, and they worked to spread awareness of her role and accomplishments during the expedition.

Honors

In 1976, she was inducted posthumously in the National Cowgirl Hall of Fame in Fort Worth, Texas. The museum is dedicated to honoring women of the American West who displayed courage and pioneering fortitude. Other honorees include the sharpshooter Annie Oakley, the novelist Willa Cather, and the first female justice of the Supreme Court, Sandra Day O'Connor.

The US Mint issued the Sacagawea dollar coin in her honor in 2000. It depicts the Shoshone guide and her baby son, Jean Baptiste. There are no contemporary images of Sacagawea, so it was decided that the image would use a modern Shoshone woman as a model. In the end, a Shoshone-Bannock woman named Randy'L He-dow Teton modeled for the engraving. Its design is considered particularly unusual as the copyright is owned solely by the US Mint, and therefore the image is not in the public domain as most images for US coinage are. When the coin's design was first debuted in 1999, First Lady Hillary Clinton remarked in her speech: "Even as she cared for her baby, she demonstrated remarkable courage and ingenuity, serving the expedition as an invaluable interpreter and guide … Sacagawea played an unforgettable role in the history of our nation."

Shortly before leaving office, in January 2001, President Bill Clinton awarded Sacagawea with the position of honorary sergeant in the regular army in thanks for her efforts during the 5,000-mile (8,000 km) expedition with Lewis and Clark.

Memorials

In addition to these honors, Sacagawea has also had numerous monuments and memorials made of her likeness or dedicated to her memory. In fact, it is believed that she may have more memorials dedicated to her than any other woman in American history. These include lakes, parks, peaks, education centers, trails, mountains, and rivers. Examples include Lake Sacajawea in Longview, Washington; the Sacajawea Memorial Area at Lemhi Pass on the boundary of Montana and Idaho; Mount Sacagawea in Fremont, Wyoming; and the Sacagawea River in Montana. Her name was even used to christen a newly discovered caldera (a large cauldron-like depression caused by the evacuation of a magma reservoir) on the planet Venus. It is known as Sacagawea Patera.

Statues of her and her infant son are almost as numerous. One of the most famous can be found in Portland, Oregon, at Washington Park. Designed by sculptor Alice Cooper in 1905, the statue depicts Sacagawea, with her son strapped to her back, pointing the way onward. Lastly, the USNS *Sacagawea*, launched in 2006, is one of several United States ships that have been named in her honor.

Legacy

The portrayal of Sacagawea through films and novels, and her elevation to the status of feminist icon, were not accidents. They were part of a wider political conflict happening within twentieth-century America. In many ways, Sacagawea became embroiled with the fight for white female rights, and as such, her image soon became wrapped up in the image of the "modern" white suffragette. The Native American princess tropes were also a part of this wider debate. These tropes were largely used by Hollywood due to inherent racism within the industry, but they would also play a part in Sacagawea's climb to feminist hero. While her actions were indeed courageous and skilled, her story was too complex for political narratives of the time. Those wishing to use her memory needed to tell the American public a much simpler story.

Depictions in Novels

Sacagawea has been a main or featured character a number of fictional novels, including *Sacajawea* by Anna Lee Waldo, *Stone Heart* by Diane Glancy, and *Streams to the River, River to the Sea* by Scott O'Dell. Some of these books have speculated about a possible romance between Sacagawea and either Clark or Lewis. However, there is no evidence of this in any of the journals and is more likely a device invented to create a more interesting story line. The concept was perhaps inspired by the highly successful 1955 Western film *The Far Horizons*,

Many novels about Sacagawea are problematic as authors often romanticize her life and infuse her story with their own ideas and agendas.

starring Charlton Heston as William Clark and Donna Reed as Sacagawea, where the pair were reimagined as lovers.

Another problematic element of many novels is the frequent descriptions of Sacagawea in terms of white beauty ideals. One of the first writers to emphasize Sacagawea's story was Eva Emery Dye. Her book was meant to be a historical account of the expedition. However, Dye often fills in missing gaps of information with her own imagination. One such example is in descriptions of Sacagawea's appearance. Dye depicts Sacagawea with "neatly braided" hair, a "fine and straight" nose, and skin of "pure copper like the statue in some old Florentine gallery." These features are more commonly associated with white beauty ideals, and the connection with Italy associates Sacagawea more with Europe than with her own people. In later books, her hair is described as a dark auburn, her eyes as grey, and her skin "a tigerish color, so light in tone that each blush was to be seen … as vividly as in the face of the fairest French or American girl." In short, Dye and other writers were trying to make Sacagawea as white as possible without losing her "exotic" Native background.

Despite this, Dye's book was one of two early twentieth-century novels that shaped the public image of Sacagawea and brought her back into the public eye after years in the historical wilderness. Dye's book, entitled *The Conquest: The True Story of Lewis and Clark*, was published in 1902, in anticipation of the expedition's centennial. Throughout the book, Sacagawea is described as a "beautiful Indian princess," a spiritual "Madonna of her race," "Indian mother," and "woman pilot," in effect constructing a romanticized role for Sacagawea within the expedition. It was a huge success and soon prompted the National American Woman Suffrage Association to embrace the Shoshone woman as a feminist hero. A flood of stories and essays appeared in ladies' magazines and journals celebrating Sacagawea's life and setting her up as a role model for the empowered American woman.

The second book to capture the public's imagination appeared some thirty years later. In 1932, historian Grace

Raymond Hebard published her biography *Sacajawea: Guide and Interpreter of Lewis and Clark* to even greater success than Dye. The book claimed to have uncovered new evidence that proved Sacagawea had in fact not died in 1812 but had escaped her husband and lived until the late 1800s. Yet, though the book found commercial success, it also attracted high-level criticism from numerous other historians who claimed that Hebard had first chosen the character she wished Sacagawea to be and then had gone in search of corroborating evidence.

Caucasian actress Donna Reed wore redface makeup to change her skin color in the 1955 film *The Far Horizons.*

Depictions in Film and Television

One of the most typical images used to depict Native American women in American media is the "Native Princess." Just like Pocahontas before her, Sacagawea would find herself transformed from a normal Shoshone girl into a Hollywood-ready princess, complete with cabaret American Indian costume. In addition, more often than not, she would be played by white or non-Native American actresses.

In one of the first film depictions of Sacagawea, the 1955 Western *The Far Horizons*, she is played by the Caucasian actress Donna Reed, wearing redface makeup to darken her skin. Publicity shots for the film depict her in classic Native princess style, with buckskin costume, smiling for the camera like a beauty queen. Since then, she has appeared as a character in many other features, including *Jefferson's West* (2003), *Bill and Meriwether's Excellent Adventure* (2006), and *The Spirit of Sacajawea* (2007). Most recently, she featured in the hugely popular Night at the Museum film series, where, perhaps unsurprisingly, the actress playing her wears a short and generic Native princess costume rather than the long and practical clothes the actual Sacagawea would most likely have worn to cover the mountainous region.

Depictions in Art

Sacagawea's image can also be found in a huge number of paintings and sculptures. Traditionally, she has been shown carrying her son, and she often is featured as part of a trio with Lewis and Clark. Most artworks have emphasized her role as a mother and as guide to the expedition by painting her pointing to somewhere just out of the picture and forging ahead of the

A statue of Sacagawea at the Buffalo Bill Center of the West in Wyoming

corps. Typically she is portrayed as conventionally attractive and smiling. Some art historians have noted how similar her images are to those created by white artists of Pocahontas, once again showing how commonly famous Native American women are reduced to American Indian princess stereotypes—beautiful, young, and helpful to white settlers.

Similar to her depiction in novels, Sacagawea has often been whitewashed in art. In one particular 1920s example, her character was used in an advertisement for the Oriental Dyeing and Cleaning Works. The photo used a model in a short and fitted Native American dress complete with a feathered headband. Media scholar Gail Guthrie Valaskasis describes the depiction as "a shapely Indian princess with perfect caucasian features." It was not enough for Sacagawea to be a legendary figure in American mythology by this point in time. In order to be palatable to a white public, any physical racial differences had to be erased.

Her sculptures have faced equal controversy. In 1976, one of the most famous statues of Sacagawea was unveiled at Fort Benton on the Missouri River. It showed her kneeling at the feet of Lewis and Clark and drew widespread protest from feminist groups, with many turning up at the monument with signs reading "Sacagawea Never Cowered!" In an attempt to counter this negative image, sculptor Harry Jackson wanted to provide a monument that moved away from sickly sweet images of Sacagawea as handmaiden. In 1980, at the Buffalo Bill Center of the West in Cody, Wyoming, a new statue was unveiled. With her blanket billowing and her hair streaming, Sacagawea was shown as a powerful and permanent figure honored in her own right. Describing the statue, historian Brian

Dippie writes, "She is no hand-maiden to white ambition; she is the earth itself."

One of the more unusual artworks that Sacagawea has found herself in ia a feminist art installation called *The Dinner Party*. Created by the artist Judy Chicago, the piece is a huge triangular table set for thirty-nine guests, all famous historical and mythological women. Along with Sacagawea, these include Sojourner Truth, Eleanor of Aquitaine, Empress Theodora of Byzantium, Virginia Woolf, Emily Dickinson, Susan B. Anthony and Georgia O'Keeffe. Each place is set with an individual hand-painted decorative cloth to reflect one of the women, ceramic flatware and a chalice, and a napkin with an embroidered gold edge. It is widely regarded as the first epic feminist artwork and was intended by the artist to serve as a symbolic history of women in Western civilization. Since 2007, it has been on permanent exhibition in the Elizabeth A. Sackler Center for Feminist Art at the Brooklyn Museum in New York.

Death and Debates

At the beginning of the twentieth century, as Sacagawea's popularity grew, more and more historians began to question whether she actually died in 1812 as previously believed. This is hardly surprising—dying at just twenty-five years old did not seem a fair or fitting end for the woman who had helped open up the West to European Americans. However, this was but a small part of a wider movement that was beginning to reexamine histories of the West and dispute the idea that Native American involvement was merely a subplot in a tale of white conquest.

Questions were raised over whether mistranslation, combined with the white men's practice of not referring to Native women by their actual names, may have affected English speakers' interpretation of who was who in the writings. This soon led to widespread academic arguments over when exactly Sacagawea had died, and in December 1924, the Bureau of Indian Affairs hired the Sioux physician and author Charles Eastman to investigate. His goal was to settle the debate between historians in Wyoming, Montana, and the Dakotas over where and when she had died.

Years before she published her research on Sacagawea's life, Grace Raymond Hebard was already petitioning Congress for funds to build a monument to Sacagawea on the Wind River Indian Reservation in Wyoming, where she believed Sacagawea had died in 1884. Herbard started gathering evidence in 1905. She trekked to find accounts among Native American oral histories and spoke to white missionaries at Wind River. She ultimately believed she had evidence that Sacagawea had managed to travel back to the Shoshones at Fort Bridger sometime in the 1850s and had lived on the reservation at Fort Washakie until she died in 1884.

Other historians, including the North Dakotan scholar Doane Robinson, insisted Hebard was incorrect and Sacagawea had in fact died in 1812. They eventually took their case to their representatives in Congress. The battle between Hebard and her opposition became so vehement that eventually the commissioner for Indian affairs called in Eastman and asked him to make an official inquiry. After interviewing Hebard's sources and the great-grandchildren of the Shoshone woman "Porivo," whom Hebard believed to have been Sacagawea,

Eastman concluded that Hebard was correct. He also stated his belief that the woman who had died at Fort Mandan in 1812 was actually Charbonneau's other Shoshone wife, Otter Woman.

As compelling as these findings seemed, there were several points of the investigation that immediately came under criticism. The majority of evidence was taken from Native American oral tradition that described women very similar to Sacagawea, but there was no real proof that these women were in fact *the* Sacagawea. Many of the stories also mentioned Charbonneau taking on two more Native American wives after his return from the expedition. This further confused matters because, in most texts, each of the four women was referred to as "Charbonneau's wife" without mentioning exact names. Furthermore, Eastman's chief witness, a Native American woman known as Mrs. Weidemann who had relayed to him an oral history passed down from her father, remarked at the end of her statement, "Some of our people say she was the same woman, others say she was not." In the end, it was almost impossible to tell if Eastman's conclusion was correct or merely hopeful.

A Feminist Icon?

After the publication of American suffragist Eva Emery Dye's *The Conquest*, Sacagawea's memory became particularly important the national suffrage movement of the 1920s. There were several reasons for this.

Sacagawea's aid to Lewis and Clark was classified as an act of patriotism and proved that patriotism could be feminine as well as something acted on by men. Sacagawea was frequently called a patriot, a name that could only truly be given to a full citizen. This lent support to the idea that citizenship was not just for men. Sacagawea's role in the Lewis and Clark expedition drew attention to women's important role in the making of a modern United States. It made sense to take a figure from America's early history in order to show how long women had been a part of shaping that history. Here was an intelligent woman, a strong mother, and an active participant in one of the most important moments in American expansion. Typically only men had been credited with establishing the West, with women often sidelined or nonexistent in tales where American heroes defeated Native Americans and tamed the West. The myth of the Western Frontier was so central to American identity that suffragists wanted to fight such stories and draw focus back to the part women played in early American settlement. As one of the few women written about from this period, Sacagawea was a natural choice. As Dye argued at the 1905 unveiling of Alice Cooper's Sacagawea statue, mentioned above, at the Lewis and Clark Exposition in Portland, Oregon:

> Women are not by nature, explorers and travelers, but where women go, homes can go, families can be reared, towns, cities, and states can be founded. Not until women came could America take any secure hold in Oregon and this great Pacific empire. With women and wagons Oregon was taken. The Indians expected to see an army with banners when the white man came, but no, the mother and child took Oregon. Trappers had been here, traders and shipmasters had skirted these wilds, but not until mothers came was

> the true seed of a nation planted. And Sacajawea led them all, the dark-eyed princess of the native race, the child of the Orient, beckoned the white man on, toward her ancient home.

While this speech might make modern feminists cringe somewhat, at the time of her speaking this was the argument that most suffragists put forward in an effort to combat the complaints of men that giving women the vote would make them too masculine. She was also trying to link the idea of Sacagawea leading Lewis and Clark to her Shoshone home with the image of white female settlers traveling westward with their families to start new lives. In this way, she fought against the idea that men forged civilization with the notion that it was instead women who paved the way. Sacagawea would later be hailed as "the first Montana suffragist." Her actions were depicted as an example of service, loyalty, and sacrifice, and they were used to show how "feminine" qualities could be applied outside of the home.

Finally, her role as a mother meant that Sacagawea was heavily portrayed in Dye's work as a "civilizing force," which supported the suffragette argument about the positive impact women could have in the world if given the vote. Dye was extremely interested in mother figures, and within her novel she modeled Sacagawea into a powerful image of pioneer motherhood. Scholar Patricia Vettel-Becker argues that Sacagawea was "an ideal prototype for the pioneering 'New Woman,' for she demonstrated that a woman could play an important role in public life without sacrificing her femininity."

The leadership role of guide that Sacagawea acquired in Dye's novel also fitted well with one of the main suffragist

Modern-Day Explorer: Osa Johnson

Osa Johnson, born Osa Helen Leighty, was an American explorer, filmmaker, and author known for her bold and daring character and her insatiable desire for new and exotic locations. In 1910, she married the travel photographer Martin Johnson, and together the pair began traveling the globe. During their travels, they made a number of documentaries with titles such as *Among the Cannibals of the South Pacific, Jungle Adventures, Headhunters of the South Seas, and Wonders of the Congo.*

While on these adventures, the Johnsons primarily worked as a team. It was Osa who would hunt for their food and stand guard with a rifle while Martin was taking photographs in dangerous locations. On one occasion, Osa brought down an enraged rhino that was charging head-on for the couple. Her quick reaction saved both their lives. Together they collected photographs and filmed the different environments they traveled through. When Osa and her husband finally returned to the United States, the couple promoted their films with a lecture tour and would later be honored with the founding of the Martin and Osa Johnson Safari Museum in their home state of Kansas. Osa would later release a memoir of her life in 1940 titled *I Married Adventure.*

arguments—how the right to vote would enable women to use their natural gifts to help guide the country toward a more civilized society. This is most clearly seen in the 1905 statue created by Alice Cooper. Vettel-Becker explains how the statue was used to promote this particular image of Sacagawea: "Cooper's noble heroine strides forcefully ahead, her chin raised, her arm lifted and pointing towards the horizon. She appears to be in vigorous motion, her buckskin garments flowing swiftly and gracefully around her, and seemingly unencumbered by the baby casually wrapped around her left shoulder." This forceful and dynamic Sacagawea combined confidence, activity, and motherhood is one easy pose.

However there was a darker side to this depiction of the mother Sacagawea as an empowered civilizing force. The real Shoshone woman underneath the legend created by Dye was not adequate in the eyes of the National American Woman Suffrage Association. In their political debate, it was white women who were the civilizing force in modern America. Thus, in order to make Sacagawea fit, her Native American identity was diminished. Descriptions of her proceeded to lighten her skin tone, make her features more European, and turn her into a Native princess of noble blood. Only the most basic suggestion of her ethnic background was left in order to suggest bravery and daring. As historian Wanda Pillow explains in her article "Searching for Sacagawea: Whitened Reproductions and Endarkened Representations": "For suffragists to use Sacagawea as an icon, her status as an Indian woman had to be erased and she had to be reassigned the attributes emblematic of white womanhood: modesty, purity, domesticity, and a keen sense of moral superiority."

Essays and articles on Sacagawea continually sought to emphasize her assimilation into white culture. In one 1903 article in the *St. Paul Globe*, she was described as "fond of white people, tried to imitate civilized ways in her dress and manners, and in general appeared like one in whom an inspiration had been aroused for something higher than savagery." This technique was primarily used to justify the colonization of the Americas by white settlers, but it also helped guarantee the security of Sacagawea's position as an inspiration for white American suffragists.

Representation Today

Today, issues of representation of Native American tribes have been once again brought to the fore under the banner of "cultural appropriation." Cultural appropriation is the adoption or use of elements of one culture by members of another, usually the use of a minority culture by a dominant, majority culture. Examples of this include Miley Cyrus's dreadlocks worn while hosting the 2015 MTV Video Music Awards and Katy Perry's geisha costume at the 2013 American Music Awards. What makes these uses problematic or offensive is how they can reshape or degrade the meaning of different symbols that play an important role in another person's culture.

Native American culture has frequently been appropriated in the past, usually in the form of films about the "Birth of the West." However, it is still an issue today. One of the most famous controversies has been the naming of NFL team the Washington Redskins. The team received the name in 1933. The term "redskin" dates back to the 1600s and is widely acknowledged as an offensive reference to a First Nations person. To add

Today, Native American dress is still appropriated by fashion, regardless of its religious or sociopolitical meaning.

further insult, the use of term redskin is connected to a time in history when bounty hunters were paid for Native people's scalps. The name is still hotly debated, with opinions among Native people ranging from support to indifference to strong opposition.

Other examples of the appropriation of Native American culture include the use of Native dress for Halloween costumes and fashion accessories. In 2012, Urban Outfitters received criticism after selling a range of "Indian" headdresses as part of their fashion accessory range. One key issue highlighted by protesters was the insult of reducing a diverse set of cultures into a fashion trend, especially in light of the long history of oppression face by Native American people. The same year, the Victoria's Secret fashion show featured a white model clad in buckskin and leopard print underwear sporting a full-length war headdress. Not only did the costume mirror sexualized images of the "Indian princess" trope, but the model even posed as if war-whooping. This was not the first time that headdresses have been used in fashion shoots

Modern-Day Interpreter: Lydia Callis

Lydia Callis rose to fame after her appearance on New York mayor Michael Bloomsberg's televised press conference. As he discussed Hurricane Sandy, the eyes of both the press and millions of viewers at home were drawn to the sight of Callis translating his speech into sign language. Her animated expressions and gestures meant the audience couldn't keep their eyes off her, and she became an overnight success. The interpreter quickly gained her own fan base, and her appearance even sparked a parody on the weekly comedy sketch show *Saturday Night Live*.

Callis grew up with sign language as her first language. Her mother and her three younger siblings were all profoundly deaf. She is, in fact, the only hearing child in three generations of her family. During her childhood and teenage years, there was almost no legal protection or assistance for the deaf or hard of hearing, and life for many of her family was a daily struggle. As an adult, she founded LC Interpreting Service, a company dedicated to providing highly trained sign language interpreters and educating the general public to deaf culture.

Callis is not only a sign language interpreter but also a community educator and advocate for equal access, working with both local and national groups to empower deaf people. She continues to work to raise awareness for deaf issues and is involved in public policy reform as well as regularly contributing to the *Huffington Post*. Her fame has helped to bring much-deserved attention to the profession of interpreting.

with a blatant disregard for their meaning. In her personal blog, the Cree writer and teacher Chelsea Vowel explains the issues behind this:

> Some items are restricted items in specific cultures. Examples from Canada and the United States would be: military medals, Bachelor degrees (the actual parchment), and certain awards representing achievement in literary, musical or other fields. These items cannot be legitimately possessed or imitated by just anyone, as they represent achievements earned according to a specific criteria … Some people will pretend to have earned these symbols, but there can be serious sanctions within a culture for doing this. For example, someone claiming to have earned a medical degree (using a fake parchment) can face criminal charges, because that "symbol" gives them access to a specialized and restricted profession … For the most part, headdresses are restricted items. In particular, the headdress worn by most non-natives imitate those worn by various Plains nations. These headdresses are further restricted within the cultures to *men* who have done certain things to earn them. It is *very* rare for women in Plains cultures to wear these headdresses, and their ability to do so is again quite restricted.
>
> So unless you are a native male from a Plains nation who has earned a headdress, or you have been given permission to wear one (sort of like being presented with an honorary degree), then you will have a very difficult time making a case for how wearing one is anything other than disrespectful, now that you know

> these things ... Even if you have "native friends" or are part native yourself, individual choices to "not be offended" do not trump our collective rights as peoples to define our symbols.

Research has shown that cultural appropriation perpetuates stereotypes harmful to Native people, severely damaging their happiness and self-esteem. In addition, exposure to these images causes people from dominant cultures, usually white Americans, to more easily believe that all First Nations people fall into the categories of violent savage, teary-eyed environmentalist, Indian princess, or casino-rich businessman.

Conclusion

Sacagawea's story has been largely one of appropriation—meaning when one group speaks for, defines, describes, represents, or uses the stories and experiences of others for their own purposes. It can also be when a person claims to be an expert on another's personal experiences. Sacagawea's story was minimized, then romanticized, and finally exaggerated. In the process, an infinitely more real, though humbler, person has been eclipsed.

While she may not be the epic heroine of Dye and Hebard's dream, Sacagawea was in her way an extraordinary person. She lived in a time of great struggle, was stolen from her family at a young age, and was constantly forced to change and adapt among strangers. She became a mother at just sixteen and then proceeded to survive and thrive on a 5,000-mile (8,000 km) trek through territory that would have been largely unknown to her. She was a peace ambassador and helped to keep a group of thirty-two men alive through her quick thinking and survival skills. She and the many other forgotten Native American women of the past deserve respect and admiration for their strength, bravery, and courage. Hopefully the continued efforts of historians and researchers will uncover further knowledge of their history.

Glossary

bilingual Able to speak two languages fluently.

colonizer A person who settles in another country and claims authority over it.

commodity A product for sale or trade.

condescending Patronizing, or showing a feeling of superiority over others.

constitutionality Accordance with the constitution of a country or state.

Enlightenment A philosophical movement of eighteenth-century Europe based on the belief in the power of reason.

Federalist An early American political party supporting a strong, centralized government.

glaciated Covered, or having been covered, by glaciers, or frozen ice sheets.

homogenous Composed of parts that are all of the same kind.

impetuosity Rash and sudden action or emotion.

indigenous Native to a particular region or country.

indispensable Absolutely necessary.

intermediary A go-between or mediator.

multilingual Using or able to speak several languages.

mythologize To idealize something or make it the subject of myth.

Native American An indigenous non-European person of North or South America or the Caribbean Islands.

pan-American Indian Across multiple Native American nations.

reconnaissance A search for useful information in the field.

romanticize To overly idealize or dramatize.

typhus An infectious disease that causes headaches and the eruption of red spots on the body.

Chronology

circa 1788 Sacagawea is born in Lemhi County, Idaho, into the Shoshone tribe.

circa 1800 Sacagawea's band is attacked by a Hidatsa band. She is captured, along with several other young girls and boys.

circa 1802 Sacagawea is given in marriage to a French Canadian fur trader named Toussaint Charbonneau.

July 1803 America purchases the Louisiana Territory from the French government. Lewis and Clark recruit men for the Corps of Discovery and prepare to set off.

November 1804 The corps arrives at the Hidatsa villages and builds Fort Mandan. Charbonneau is hired as a interpreter, and he and Sacagawea move into the fort. She is now pregnant with her first child.

February 1805 Sacagawea gives birth to a son named Jean Baptiste, assisted by Lewis.

April 1805 The expedition leaves Fort Mandan and begins the journey up the Missouri River.

May 1805 One of the expedition's boats overturns in the water and important items are swept away. Sacagawea quickly retrieves the items, earning the praise of the captains. Lewis names the river Sacagawea in her honor.

June 1805 Sacagawea becomes severely sick for ten days.

August 1805 Sacagawea recognizes Beaverhead Rock and leads the expedition to a Shoshone band. They meet with the band and discovered its leader is Sacagawea's brother.

November 1805 The group finally reaches the Pacific Ocean and builds their winter fort.

March 1806 The corps heads home.

August 1806 They arrive back at Fort Mandan, and Sacagawea and her family leave the group.

October 1810 Sacagawea moves to St. Louis with her family.

March 1811 Sacagawea and Charbonneau move to Fort Manuel Lisa, leaving Jean Baptiste in Clark's care.

August 1812 Sacagawea gives birth to a daughter named Lizette.

December 1812 Sacagawea allegedly dies of typhus.

circa 1875 A woman living on the Wind River Reservation claims to be Sacagawea.

April 1884 The woman claiming to be Sacagawea dies.

November 1976 Sacagawea is inducted into the National Cowgirl Hall of Fame.

November 1999 First official striking of the Sacagawea US dollar.

January 2001 President Bill Clinton gives Sacagawea the title of Honorary Sergeant, Regular Army.

Further Information

Books

Clark, Ella E., and Margot Edmonds. *Sacagawea of the Lewis and Clark Expedition*. Berkeley: University of California Press, 1983.

Rogers, Sam. *What's So Great About Sacagawea?* KidLit-O Press, 2014.

Summit, April R. *Sacagawea: A Biography*. Westport, CT: Greenwood Press, 2008.

Films

Burns, Ric, Sarah Colt, Dustinn Craig, and Mark Zwonitzer. *We Shall Remain*. Directed by Ric Burns, Sarah Colt, Dustinn Craig, Chris Eyre, and Stanley Nelson. Arlington, VA: PBS, 2009.

Native American history over the last three hundred years is explored in this PBS mini-series.

Duncan, Dayton. *Lewis & Clark: The Journey of the Corps of Discovery*. Directed by Ken Burns. Arlington, VA: PBS, 1997.

Two episodes of the Ken Burns series "American Lives" tell the story of the entire Corps of Discovery.

Websites

Lewis & Clark National Historic Trail

https://www.nps.gov/lecl/index.htm

This National Park Service site features interactive maps and suggested trails for visitors to plan a visit and retrace the expedition's path.

PBS: Sacagawea

http://www.pbs.org/lewisandclark/inside/saca.html

An in-depth look inside the Corps of Discovery and at the life story of Sacagawea. Includes an interactive trail map and classroom resources.

President Jefferson and the Indian Nations

https://www.monticello.org/site/jefferson/president-jefferson-and-indian-nations

Analysis of President Jefferson's attitude and policies towards Native American people during his presidency.

Bibliography

Bruchac, Joseph. *Sacajawea: The Story of Bird Woman and the Lewis and Clark Expedition.* New York: Scholastic Inc, 2001.

Buchanan, Paul D. *The American Women's Rights Movement.* Wellesley: Branden Books, 2009.

Carosella, Melissa & Stephanie Kuligowski. *Founding Mother: Women Who Shaped America.* Huntingdon Beach: Teacher Created Materials, 2012.

Clark, Ella Elizabeth. *Indian Legends of the Pacific Northwest.* Berkeley: University of California Press, 2003.

Clark, Ella Elizabeth, and Margot Edmonds. *Sacagawea of the Lewis and Clark Expedition.* Berkeley: University of California, 1983.

Dye, Eva Emery. *The Conquest: The True Story of Lewis and Clark.* Chicago: A. C. Mcclure & Company, 1902.

Gaffney, Dennis. '"American Indian" or "Native American"?' PBS.org, April 24, 2006. http://www.pbs.org/wgbh/roadshow/fts/bismarck_200504A16.html.

Green, Rayna. "The Pocahontas Perplex: The Image of Indian Women in American Culture." *Massachusetts Review* 16 (1975): 698–714.

Jager, Rebecca Kay. *Malinche, Pocahontas, and Sacagawea: Indian Women as Cultural Intermediaries and National Symbols.* Norman: University of Oklahoma Press, 2015.

Lewis, Meriwether and William Clark. *The Journals of Lewis and Clark.* Washington, DC: National Geographic Society, 2002.

McMurtry, Larry. *Sacagawea's Nickname: Essays on the American West.* New York: New York Review Books, 2004.

Nelson, W. Dale. *Interpreters with Lewis and Clark: The Story of Sacagawea and Toussaint Charbonneau.* Denton: University of North Texas Press, 2003.

Perdue, Theda, ed. *Sifters: Native American Women's Lives.* New York: Oxford University Press, 2001.

Pillow, Wanda. "Searching for Sacajawea: Whitened Reproductions and Endarkened Representations." *Hypatia* 22 (2007): 1–19.

Ronda, James P. *Lewis and Clark: Among the Indians.* Lincoln: University of Nebraska Press: 2014.

Scharff, Virginia. *Twenty Thousand Roads: Women, Movement, and the West.* Berkley: University of California Press, 2003.

Vettel-Becker, P. "Sacagawea and Son: The Visual Construction of America's Maternal Feminine." *American Studies* 50 (2009): 27–50.

Index

Page numbers in **boldface** are illustrations. Entries in **boldface** are glossary terms.

About the Author

Katie Griffiths is a long-time enthusiast of history from around the world. Her love of different cultures and their stories has taken her to many countries, including China, Japan, and Cambodia. She currently lives in Edinburgh, Scotland. She loves traveling, hiking, and collecting graphic novels in her free time. To learn more and see her other works, visit www.katiegriffiths.org.